A WINGLESS HOPE

A THUMBELINA RETELLING

A WINGLESS HOPE

A THUMBELINA RETELLING

SYDNEY WINWARD

A Wingless Hope: *A Thumbelina Retelling*

Cover art by Kayla Eshbaugh

Published by Silver Forge Books

Ebook ISBN: 978-1-960461-09-4

Paperback ISBN: 978-1-960461-12-4

http://www.sydneywinward.com

To the amazing group of authors I got to work with in this fun series and meaningful project! I've enjoyed the entire process of bringing this book to life.

BOOKS BY SYDNEY WINWARD

The Bloodborn Series
Bloodborn
Bloodbond
Bloodscourge
Bloodbane
Bloodcurse
Bloodheir

Letters to Love Series
Yours, Sterling
Forever, Mirabelle
Always, Ivette
Charles, With Love

**Sunlight and Shadows
Series**
A Breath of Sunlight
A Taste of Shadows
A Glimpse of Music
A Kiss of Embers
A Balm of Healing

Novellas
Through Wylder
Meadows
Root Brew Float
On Silver Wings
Bloodmoon
Selkie
A Wingless Hope

CHAPTER ONE

THERE WAS NOTHING enjoyable about being a prince. Nothing at all.

Not the stuffy people or the fake laughter or the appearances he had to put up to make it seem as if he was happy to be there, to give the rest of his life away to a princess who hadn't even sprouted yet.

Six-year-old Quinn Thistlethorn, heir to the Thistlethorn crown, scowled at the shimmering, golden seed the size of his head resting on top of lush, green ferns. Sunlight cascaded through the window, and an awe-filled sigh escaped more than one mouth in the room.

Tomorrow, the seed would be planted, and in a few months, her flower would sprout before the pixie would emerge from the petals.

But today…

They would be bonded.

His scowl deepened at the terrible thought.

"She's beautiful." King Florian Firewillow gazed down at his daughter still in the seed. "I have not seen a lovelier gem in all my life."

The adults drawled on and on about the rarest seed to be laid in the past two hundred years—a goldenblush briar. A fitting flower for such a monumental task as bringing peace between their people.

Quinn glanced toward the window of the enormous palace tree in wistful silence. He longed to spread his purple translucent wings beneath the moonlight, to feel the air rushing through his ebony hair, to be *anywhere* but fawning over something that hadn't even sprouted yet.

"Don't you think she's lovely, Quinn?" his father asked, forcefully pulling his attention back to the boring conversation with the other adults in the room consisting of his father, older sister Cassie, and the pixie king and queen of Mapleborough and their son near his age, Gabriel.

Quinn stared blankly at his father. "She's a seed."

Citron Thistlethorn, king of Shadowfalls and also his father, chuckled nervously before gripping him tight on the shoulder. A silent warning. "She is your betrothed. When she comes of age, you two will marry and unite our two kingdoms, ending this war once and for all."

Yuck.

He coughed behind his hand if only to hide the way he stuck his tongue out at the seed. She didn't even have a name yet and she was already ruining his plans to run far away from home and never return. He didn't like being a prince. He wanted the freedom of the skies and the excitement of adventure. Someday, he was going to be the fastest pixie to ever fly in the lands of Eliandor. He certainly wasn't going to marry some girl who would sprout without wings, anyway. Because the pixies of Mapleborough had no wings unlike his own people.

The queen of Mapleborough stroked the shimmering surface of the seed and smiled softly. "We will name her Briar after her rare bloom. Briar Firewillow. The only princess to be born to our family thus far."

And the only one that ever will be, everyone else likely thought because they've said it an infuriating number of times behind their backs. Quinn couldn't understand why it took so long for them to have a seed in the first place. And he didn't understand why they wouldn't have more, either.

"Are you ready?" his father asked, guiding him forward with a sturdy hand that felt more like a prison than a loving touch.

He huffed as he pleaded with his eyes alone. The silence roared in his ears, and even when he spoke quietly, it was as if his voice echoed off the walls of the tree palace. "I don't want to."

His father crouched to his level, took him by the shoulders, and looked him in the eye. To others it might have appeared as if he offered reassurance. But to him, it was another warning.

"Quinn, someday you will rule Shadowfalls, and my magic will pass down the line to you. You will be taxed with the great responsibility of protecting the pixies within our borders. But you cannot do it alone." He gestured to Briar's seed. "Uniting our kingdoms is not just for peace but for safety as well. She will hold half of the magic and you the other half. It creates a much-needed balance for our forest."

The open window pulled his attention away from his father's warning stare. He could still fly away. He didn't have to be the one to have so much responsibility on his shoulders. He didn't have to mourn his mother anymore.

He could be free.

But his father's grip tightened on his shoulders, and he tore his gaze away from the window, away from freedom, and fixed his moody stare on the shimmery seed. *Briar Firewillow.*

I hate you, he internally seethed, and he promised to hate her until the day he found his freedom. Because after this ceremony, after everyone went to bed at the crack of dawn and only the sentries were out guarding his kingdom, he would disappear. Forever.

As the fire of anger crackled through his veins, he placed his hand on top of the seed, his purple-gray skin and black fingernails a stark contrast to the golden shimmer.

Within moments, as if afraid Quinn might pull away, the Mapleborough warlock approached quickly from the shadows and hovered his own hand over the two of them. Close but not touching.

"With my magic, I bind you, Quinn Thistlethorn of Shadowfalls and Briar Firewillow of Mapleborough as intendeds, as future bondmates of souls and magic. To share power. To act as one. To protect and serve our people. To protect each other with your very life. And now…" He touched each of them with the tip of his finger. "You are bound."

Quinn hissed at the sharp sting enveloping his wrist and climbing up his forearm. He snatched his hand away, his eyes wide as he watched as a green, leafy vine design etched itself into his skin. It meant Briar's eyes would be green. And when she was planted and later sprouted, her wrist would sport a matching mark a violet in color to match his eyes.

He scrubbed his arm on his trousers, but all he managed was to irritate his skin. The mark remained.

"Oh, how wonderful," the queen sighed happily. "Our people are waiting. Let's announce the good news."

"There's nothing good about it," he grumbled quietly to himself.

Unfortunately, his father heard and grabbed him by the arm, pulling him after the others through the large, hollowed-out living tree palace. Quinn glared at the paintings on the walls crafted of leaf pulp canvas and berry paint. He glared at the series of winding corridors weaving through the enormous tree. And he continued to glare as they stepped outside on a wooden balcony overlooking thousands of wingless pixies below. Large trees surrounded the palace grounds, stretching almost as high as the sun itself. Flowers at least five times the size of each pixie dotted the ground in pinks, yellows, whites, and more. And far down below, he spotted a large fountain parting the sea of pixies with spurting water. The water cascaded from a stone pixie's trumpet, her dress wrapped around her legs as if an imaginary wind blew through the glade.

At the sight of both royal families, the crowd below roared with excitement, the blaring sound attacking his ears and making him want to recoil to somewhere quiet and void of bright, cheery people. This was the second worst day of his life, the first being when his mother had been killed by goblins. Why was everyone so happy?

"Stop looking glum," his father hissed at the side of his mouth. "Give them a wave."

But Quinn had obeyed one too many commands already and refused to lift a hand. He didn't even care to smile.

The king of Mapleborough raised a hand, and the crowd quieted below. The man's gentle hand on his back was a stark contrast to his own father's strong, relentless grip. He led Quinn forward as if to give his subjects a better view of him.

"I am honored to announce the betrothal of my daughter, Briar, to the strapping lad, Quinn

Thistlethorn!" More roars and rounds of applause. Everyone was eager for the war and bloodshed between their people to end.

Quinn scowled. Their departure from this awful, bright kingdom couldn't come soon enough.

And as was customary with betrothals, his father handed him to the king of Mapleborough, and the king handed Briar's seed to his father to signify something boring that he couldn't care to pay attention to. Rather, he slyly glanced around to give himself something to do other than listen to boring adult things.

His eyebrows furrowed when he spotted a red-robed figure standing behind them partially hidden behind the door, their face shrouded by a hood. These pixies sure did dress strangely in their light-colored garb. The pixies from Shadowfalls often wore black or other dark colors. But never flamboyant red. Only ritual warlocks wore such clothing.

But then his heart froze when he caught the sheen of metal sticking out from beneath the robe. Was the robed person a guard? Surely, they must be if they had managed to enter the palace at all, as it was heavily guarded all the time.

He returned his attention to the skies ahead of him, watching as a bird flew over the tops of the trees. He envied their freedom. But he vowed that someday, he would fly to the moon.

Red flashed in the corner of his eye. Time seemed to slow as the figure in the robe withdrew their dagger. In a blurred motion, they thrust their weapon through his father's back from behind.

His father grunted. Quinn's eyes widened with horror.

And then his father stumbled forward as if losing control of his body. He crashed into the balcony. The seedling flew from his arms and over the side of the railing. The queen screamed. Shadowfalls guards jumped into action.

Quinn reacted quickly, almost instinctively, as all the hate for the seed melted away into panic. His brand on his arm burned, urging him to react.

He didn't stop to think of the possible consequences of his actions as he dove over the side of the railing and flattened his wings against his body to give him a burst of speed. Wind whipped through his hair as the ground came at him at an alarming rate. He held his hands outstretched toward the falling seedling.

For a moment, he feared he would not catch it. She would not survive a fall from such a height.

His fingers skimmed the golden seed. The ground came even closer. And finally, he grabbed hold of the seed and braced her against his chest in the safety of his arms. However, he couldn't slow his descent fast enough to protect himself.

He twisted to the side only a moment before he crashed into the fountain below with a deafening splash. His body thudded against the bottom. Agonizing pain seared his back. His chest ached with the need for air, but for a moment, he couldn't move. The fall had stunned him.

But then the distorted ripples of something red above the surface kicked his heart into a panic.

His head broke the surface of the fountain, and he gasped for air. Screams assaulted his ears. Weapon clashing against weapon lifted into the skies. Soldiers fought against dozens of red-robed figures. Pixies ran away from the impending threat, which only created more disorienting chaos surrounding him.

A red-robed figure stood over the fountain with his dagger raised directly above Quinn's head. The figure thrust downward. Quinn ducked out of the way of the attack. And then he flipped over the lip of the fountain and scrambled toward the safety of the forest, dripping wet with the seedling in his arms.

Against a plethora of pixies without the ability to fly, he knew he had the advantage. But as he tried to spread his wings, pain ripped across his back once more. They refused to obey him.

They were too wet, he decided. He had to use his legs for now.

Quinn weaved in and out of taller pixies running for their lives. A much larger man bumped into him, and he fell to the ground, barely managing to brace himself against the impact with one hand.

His pained, exhausted body wanted to give up. But to give up meant to either get trampled or stabbed. So, he scrambled to his feet and ran as fast as his legs would carry him.

He darted into blades of grass taller than himself with the robed figure at his heels, quickly losing the man in the thick, woodsy foliage. His heart thundered. His lungs gasped for breath. He didn't know where he was going. He couldn't see the path ahead. All he knew was he needed to keep running. To keep moving. To keep the seedling safe.

Although he knew he should keep himself safe instead, he felt compelled to protect the seed. His burning brand seemed to tell him so.

Just as he leaped over a small stream of water, someone tackled him from behind.

An alarmed cry escaped him. The seed flew from his arms. Dirt and rocks scraped against his hands. The breath got knocked from his lungs, making him unable to cry for help. He flopped onto his back, eyes wide when he found another robed figure with his wicked dagger poised above him.

Quinn threw his arms up to protect himself and squeezed his eyes shut, bracing himself for the bite of the blade. But it never came.

He glanced up to find a Mapleborough sentry behind the man with his sword thrust into the enemy's back from behind, the tip of the weapon protruding from the man's chest.

The enemy dropped his weapon. The metal dagger clattered to the rocky floor. The man pitched forward and crashed into the ground.

The sentry stepped forward. Quinn clambered backward and rolled onto his feet. But as he tried to lift his wings to fly away from the imposing threat, his back screamed in protest. And only then did he glance behind him.

His heart fell to the very pit of his stomach. The left side of his wings were damp but intact. But the right side…

His forewing… It was broken. Cracked. Tattered.

And he'd seen enough injuries in Shadowfalls to know he would never fly again.

Tears filled his eyes, blurring the sentry holding the bloodied sword at his side. For a moment, he couldn't think about Briar's seed. He couldn't think about the risk to his life when all he saw were the bright skies overhead, now forever out of reach. He would never again feel the freedom of the skies. Never feel the wind in his hair and the moonlight against his face.

He was grounded.

For good.

He was never going to fly again.

A sob escaped him, from both pain and the misery of being grounded. His body hurt too much to run again, even as the sentry approached.

"Shh, shh, shh," the man with tanned skin and graying curls tried to soothe. He placed his sword on the ground and approached with a cautious hand held toward him. "My name is Matthias. I'm here to aid you." He noticed Quinn's shredded wing and inhaled sharply. "We'll get you help. I promise." And then he glanced over his head. "Where's Briar's seed?"

Quinn swiped the tears from his eyes and glanced behind him. But the seed had disappeared, the golden shimmer nowhere in sight.

At least until the caw of a blue jay chilled his blood. Moments later, a golden sheen pulled his attention to the seedling in the beak of a bird five times his size. The sentry shouted at the creature and tried to run toward it, but the bird took flight, the gold catching on the sunlight moments before the blue jay disappeared, taking Briar with him.

After everything…Quinn had failed to keep the princess safe.

And if a bird had the seed, it was unlikely anyone would see it again.

But a fragile hope took a hold of him when he spotted Shadowfalls guards darting after the bird through the skies. Perhaps all hope was not lost. Not yet.

As the shock slowly faded away, the burning pain from his broken wing collapsed him to his knees. He didn't run, didn't fight as the sentry picked him up in his arms and took him back to the palace.

A half dozen enemies in red robes lay lifeless. The other half were nowhere to be seen within the vicinity, as if they had fled when their adversary proved too strong to contend with.

A head of black hair stood out amidst light-colored locks, drawing his attention to his father sitting with his back against the fountain, dozens of people surrounding him, including a physician. He, too, must have fallen over the railing. But his wings could have saved him from the deadly impact.

His father's head lolled to the side as he met Quinn's eye, the movement revealing the blood soaked into his black clothing.

Quinn thrashed out of the sentry's arms, ignoring the pain pulsing through his back as he rushed toward his father, pushing someone's legs aside to move them out of his way before kneeling beside him.

"Papa!" Quinn choked, his attention darting from the large, bloody wound in his abdomen to the blood escaping the corner of his mouth. "Papa!"

His father's fingers trembled as he clasped his hand and gave it a feeble squeeze. "My power will transfer to you," he rasped. "Use it wisely, little Quinn. Our people will look to you for guidance."

"Don't go. Don't go!"

But his father said nothing more as one final breath escaped his lips, and the light left his eyes. And then his body lay still.

Quinn sat back on his heels, staring at his father's body in shock. He felt the very moment the life left him, as a powerful surge of magic rushed into him, growing larger and more powerful with each shaky inhale of his breath. The power burned dark and hot like the moon burning in the night sky, filling every speck of his body until even his fingernails were infused with the powerful magic of his ancestors.

Despite the raw power churning within him, numbness crawled through his chest. His father was gone. His wing was broken. He didn't know how to be king.

And later, he'd learn that they never found the princess.

In a single day, he'd lost everything. And he had no idea how he could possibly go forward with nothing.

CHAPTER TWO

Nineteen years later

THE WORLD WAS TOO big for a tiny little person like Briar. Leaving the safety of her flower never ended well, no matter how cautious she was when her curiosity about the outside world set in. Especially today.

She gasped for each heaving, burning breath as she sprinted through sticky marshland. Her bare feet slopped through thick, unforgiving mud. Brambles snagged the sack of a dress she wore from scraps she'd found from a bird's nest. The knots in her golden hair tangled further when wind whipped the gnarled strands around her face.

"Ah!" she cried out as she stumbled over a slimy stick hidden in the mud and crashed into a murky puddle of water.

Her pulse thrummed faster and faster as she clawed through the mud to try to dislodge her leg. When a ferocious hiss and scampering feet sounded behind her, she stretched with every muscle in her body to reach for an overhanging vine. Her fingers missed her first attempt, but when the rat skidded around the corner and bared its four sharp teeth, she reached again, this time grabbing a hold.

With all her might, she pulled herself out of the mud. But with a *slop*, her leg dislodged all too quickly, and the momentum sprang her into the air.

Her hold on the vine slipped, and she screamed again when a rush of blue skies and green swampland blurred in her vision moments before she crashed into a batch of brightly colored tulips.

The soft leaves caught her fall, but the landing still made her dazed and dizzy. Something large crashed through the foliage behind her, and she stumbled to her feet. The world tipped and spun as she ran, but she didn't get far before exhaustion swooped her legs out from beneath her, and she hit the hard dirt road with a thud.

Briar curled into a ball, bracing herself for the rat's painful bite.

But rather than becoming rodent food, the creature hissed and squealed before falling quiet.

Alarm flitted through her chest as she sat up suddenly to find a white and pink tabby cat dropping the large, dead rat into a bush. The creature rounded on her, slinking forward with intelligent blue eyes sparkling with interest.

"Please!" she begged, trying to remain as still as possible to deter the cat from chasing her. "Spare me. Please."

"Ohhh," the cat purred, followed by a *tsk* as she sat back on her haunches and tipped her head to the side. "You look like you've had a rough time of it. What has you so afraid?"

Briar's jaw hung agape when she realized this was no ordinary cat. It could speak unlike any cat she'd ever known. And its first instinct wasn't to bat her around like the last feline she'd encountered.

The last fragile emotion broke as tears escaped from her eyes and ran down her face. Her words were hardly discernible when she spoke quickly and blubbered every sentence. "The frog down by the river tried to drag me away, and when I escaped, the rat found me and chased me all the way from my flower to…to…" Her shoulders slumped when she didn't recognize her surroundings. She was hopelessly lost when the world around her was just too big. "Here!" she finally cried with a gesture to her surroundings. "I'm so lost and so alone. I can't survive by myself anymore! I don't want to be alone."

Because the moment she had emerged from her flower years ago, she had been alone. As far as she knew, she was the only one of her kind. She looked similar to a human, but humans compared to her were giants.

The cat's purr increased in volume as she licked her paw and batted her tail calmly against the ground. "Oh, dear child. This is why Laelynn is here to help."

"Laelynn?"

"Mmmhmm. My name." The cat turned in a circle, her tail brushing against her shoulder and nearly knocking her over with the strength behind it. "Who gave you *your* name?"

Briar wiped the tears from her face and stood on shaky legs. "My flower whispered it to me. I know nothing else of my origins." She winced when her entire body, including her hair, was caked in mud. Life had been so very hard and unkind to her, even when she tried to be kind to others.

But surely things would look up for her. One of these days, she would find her own purpose.

Laelynn stretched and withdrew her claws, sharpening them on the nearby tree towering over them. Sunlight broke through the flowering leaves, the scent of new blossoms filling the skies with their sweet yet putrid stench.

"Your flower is too hidden, little Briar," the cat said, brushing her tail along her shoulder again. This time, she stumbled backward and wind-milled her arms to maintain her balance. "It needs to move."

She outstretched her hands and shrugged pitifully. "How? It's much too large and heavy. And I don't want to draw attention to myself."

"But that's precisely what you must do." She purred and leaped onto the lowest branch of the tree. Briar had to crane her neck to see her. "Draw attention to yourself."

To move her flower posed a terrible risk. Because should her flower die, she would die, too. Like learning her name, her flower had whispered the harsh truths of the world to her. She didn't know how the golden bloom became planted beside the river, but moving it didn't seem to be in her best interest.

Laelynn draped her tail over the side of the branch, and it swung slowly back and forth as she basked in the intermittent sunlight. Although she was a cat, something about her felt safe and welcoming, not at all threatening.

"If you cannot move it yourself…" The cat's twinkling blue eyes turned and blinked at something behind her. Briar followed her gaze, standing on her toes to peer over the side of a large blade of grass. But then the blood rushed from her face when she realized where she was.

A human house made of straw and brick loomed high in front of her, casting a shadow over what appeared to be a well-manicured garden. From her vantage point, she couldn't see much of anything else unless she climbed higher. And currently, she had no leftover strength to climb anything.

"A human?" she hissed, lowering her voice as if doing so could hide her from listening ears. "They will sooner squash me than help me."

But Laelynn only closed her eyes and rested her pink and white head on the branch, her fur rippling lightly in the breeze. "I thought I saw something interesting around the corner. Perhaps you should take a look yourself."

Briar glanced toward the brick path, her curiosity winning over her fear. It couldn't hurt learning what the cat spoke of. Despite their short acquaintance, she didn't think Laelynn would do anything to harm her.

Her attention returned to the tree branch, and her heart jolted in surprise to find it bare. The cat had disappeared as if she hadn't existed in the first place.

Briar placed a hand to her head, briefly wondering if the fall had rattled her brains a bit too hard. Could Laelynn have been a fairy? They were different from pixies, usually much larger, and had their own interests at heart. But the cat hadn't seemed malicious at all. Rather, she'd genuinely seemed as if she'd wanted to help.

Straightening her muddy skirts and tossing her stiff, dirty hair over her shoulder, she started down the path. "All right, kitty. What is so interesting that you believe I must see?"

The dusty scent of a cornfield mixed with the floral scents of spring in the air as she cautiously ambled down the pathway. She jumped over large cracks in the stones and avoided splashing in puddles of mud or water. Several birds flew overhead, and to avoid their notice, she ducked closer to the side of the path where marigolds and tulips, daisies and roses extended over their flower bed as if to reach out to an old friend.

When she rounded the bend in the path, she halted in her tracks and gasped. A tiny little house three times her height lay within a garden of daffodils, easily missed by a human who might be passing by, but she spotted it instantly as small as she was. The house was made of wood, painted in greens, pinks, and reds with a wooden roof on top created to look like leaves. Several small windows were carved into the sides of the house while a door with a curved top lay open. Almost like an invitation.

Briar glanced back and forth across the path, and finding it empty, she dared to venture closer to the beautiful house.

"Hello?" she called, craning her neck to find out if the house was occupied. But no one answered back.

She approached cautiously and ran a hand over the grooves etched into the wood to mimic tree bark. A small lantern hung from a hook beside the door, and when she touched it, it squeaked as it swung back and forth.

A part of her knew she shouldn't venture any farther, but her curiosity won over yet again as she peeked her head inside the house.

She gasped again.

The walls were painted with a beautiful pink and yellow flowery pattern with green vines stretching across one side of the curved structure to the other. She marveled at the chair tucked into a table and the bed with flowery sheets to match the walls.

By the time she stopped to admire the moving chair beside a fire painted on the wall, she realized she'd stepped fully into the house and now stood on a circular rug knitted with colorful yarn. Her fingers smoothed over the soft rug, and she marveled once more that such a beautiful thing could lie empty. Did someone already live here? Were they gone and planned to return home soon?

"Gotcha!" someone exclaimed loudly, followed by the door slamming closed behind her.

Briar yelped when the house tipped one way and then the other, and she struggled to stay on her feet as the structure swayed until she lost her balance entirely and fell onto the rug.

On her hands and knees, she scrambled toward one of the windows and tried to squeeze through one of the four panes, but she was much too big to fit. But then her heart squeezed with panic when she noticed the house was no longer on the ground. It swayed back and forth as the outside world disappeared, replaced by larger wooden walls and furniture decorating the inside of a human home.

Each step to the next level of the house jarred her, and she grabbed onto the windowpane slats to keep from getting flung into the hazards the furniture in the smaller house provided.

Another door slammed closed, and the impact of the house dropping onto a table jarred her enough to lose her grip on the window and crash onto the ground.

She rubbed her hip, wincing at what was bound to leave a bruise by the time she woke up the next morning.

Unexpectedly, the door of the house flew open, and a large blue eye appeared moments later.

Briar screamed and scrambled backward on her hands and feet until her back hit the corner of the bed frame. Her chest heaved with each fearful breath. Her hands felt behind her for anything she could use as a weapon. But everything was either bolted down or not sharp enough to be of use.

"Don't be afraid, little pixie," the girl's voice said as she stepped away from the house as if to give her space. "You are safe here."

And then her heart jolted for an entirely different reason, and she forgot her fear entirely. "What did you say?"

She climbed to her feet and rushed toward the door, peeking only her head out to find a little girl—a *large* little girl, a human—watching her with big blue eyes filled with excitement. She wore a white and blue dress with blue bows tied at the end of either braid, the skirts fanning out around her legs as she twisted back and forth as if hardly able to contain herself.

"I said you are safe here."

Taking a single step out of the house, she shook her head. "You called me a pixie."

"That's what you are!" The girl frowned. "Though, what happened to your wings?"

"Wings?" She glanced behind her with a puzzled frown. "I don't have any wings."

The girl's frown deepened. "Oh, what a shame." She held up a finger and rushed from the room, only to return quickly with a small bathtub filled with water. She stirred it with her finger, and it created bubbles within.

"You are filthy, pixie. Take a bath, and I'll find you new clothes!"

The girl crossed the room and dug into a large, wooden chest. Briar eyed the water suspiciously. Although the girl had captured her, she didn't seem malicious. Rather, it was as if she wanted to help her rather than harm her.

And she realized with a discouraging ache that she needed help. She wasn't safe on her own. She could not keep getting by with no one to help her when surrounded by such a large world.

She made a quick decision and stripped off her ragged clothing and dipped herself into the tub. She sighed at the luxurious warmth of the water, as she'd never bathed anywhere but in cold puddles beside the river.

A small, white blob rested on the ledge of the tub, and when she grabbed it, it slipped out of her hands and beneath the water. Soap! She'd heard about soap before, but never had she seen it in person.

She giggled as she scrubbed her body clean and next, her hair, the water slowly turning from clear to muddy brown. The girl returned and helped her into a cloth to dry herself and spread out a variety of dresses on the table beside the tub. Briar inhaled sharply at the beautiful gowns her very own size. One with ruffles like a daffodil. Another pink and shimmery like a rose. Several more that made her feel as if she were surrounded by a beautiful garden. It was almost as if the girl had waited for her arrival.

"I made them to work with pixie wings, but I'm sure they will still fit you," the girl explained. "Go on. Pick whatever you like."

Choosing between the wide variety of dresses proved difficult because they were far more luxurious than what she'd ever worn before. She stepped carefully between the fabrics, making sure not to brush against any of them, afraid a simple touch might ruin them. She stopped to admire a filmy light blue dress with a yellow sash. The creamy yellow hue reminded her of the inner petals of her goldenblush bloom waiting for her beside the river.

She perked up at the thought. Laelynn had said she needed to find someone to move her flower. What about this human girl?

As she dressed while the girl turned her back, the girl asked as if attuned to her thoughts, "Where is your flower, little pixie?"

Briar bit her tongue with concentration as she tied the yellow sash behind her back. And unable to help herself, she twirled, giggling as she watched the skirts fan out around her. "My name is Briar. And it's by the river. A golden bloom." And then she twirled again. "Oh, this is lovely. Thank you so much!"

"I made them myself! I'm Priscilla. And wait right here. I'm going to move your flower to our garden."

Priscilla rushed out of the room, braids flying behind her. Briar took that opportunity to explore her new surroundings. The small cottage her size lay on top of a table, but the drop to the floor was so steep that she avoided skirting the edges to prevent herself from falling.

Pieces of parchment lay scattered on one side of the table, and she hefted each page to the side to find colorful drawings of people her own size.

But with wings…

One of the drawings had black hair and purplish skin with the most beautiful purple, glittering wings. A pit of longing welled in her chest as she laid beside the drawing and traced the wings belonging to the man, and then she traced his purplish, pointed ears peeking out of his hair.

He looked so…*similar* to her. Of course, her skin was a lighter shade of pink like the human's, but her ears were pointed and her body small.

Excitement alighted within her as she climbed to her feet.

"A pixie!" she exclaimed as she located a blue ribbon to match her dress and tied her hair back, so the long, golden strands tumbled to her waist. "I never even realized." Especially because she didn't have wings.

But what now? Now that she knew *what* she was, could she find out *who* she was? Where did the pixies live? Why had she never seen one until these drawings?

She scoffed and rolled her eyes at herself. Laelynn was right. Her flower had been too secluded, too alone. Of course, she'd overheard other creatures and humans talking near the river, which was why she knew as much as she did, including the language she spoke. But not once had she actually seen a pixie.

The violet birthmark circling her left forearm drew her attention, and she traced the intricate leaf-like designs with the tip of her finger. She had a feeling deep in her gut that her birthmark told of her identity. But even her flower couldn't reveal who she was or where she needed to go.

Or why she had been abandoned by the side of the river.

If there were other pixies out there like her, why had she always been so alone?

She recalled what her flower had whispered to her over the years, that she had emerged from her flower as a baby. But with no one to take care of her, the flower had pulled her back into its petals and provided her with comfort and sustenance.

One of Briar's earliest memories consisted of squinting at the sunlight as she emerged again from her flower years later, learning how to cope and survive on her own. Those had been dreadful years. Lonely. Difficult. But at least her flower had closed its petals over her each winter to help her survive the harsh elements when unable to provide for herself.

At least until she grew older.

"It's all right," she said cheerily as she fought against the heartache swelling within her chest. "I am happy. It does not matter who I could have been."

A sudden, powerful surge of fatigue collapsed Briar to her hands and knees, and she found herself gasping for air. She clawed at her throat when it felt as if her lungs were blocked. Every limb in her body felt weighed down as if someone shoveled dirt on top of her until the weight threatened to collapse her entirely. Her body screamed in agony, pulling against taut threads until she feared she might combust.

Just as quick as the sudden onslaught of agony, it disappeared as a wave of normalness washed through her. She gasped in breath after breath, her eyes fluttering closed in relief. Never in her life had she felt as if she were suffocating with no way to draw air into her body.

Likely because…

Her flower had never been moved before.

She scrambled toward the window above the table, heaving herself onto the small ledge before peering outside. Down below in the garden, Priscilla tucked her flower into the dirt and sprinkled water over its golden petals with a tin watering can.

Immediately, Briar felt a cool rush of relief wash over her when the roots of her flower found the sustenance it needed to keep strong and steady.

The pounding of footsteps on the stairs reverberated in her ears, and moments later, Priscilla returned, breathless and a face flushed red. "Now you can stay forever!" she exclaimed. "I will make the most beautiful gowns for you, and we can have tea parties and dress up and, oh, we'll have so much fun together!"

A second pair of footsteps on the stairs sounded heavier than the last, and Briar's stomach twisted in alarm when a man with rounded ears and a full brown beard entered the room next. With one sweeping glance, he took in the small cottage, Briar, and the dresses laid out on the table.

He sighed. "What did I tell you about keeping pixies as pets? How long have you had this one for?"

"I found her today, Papa. Can I keep her? Please?"

The man crouched until his face was eye level with her. He was a giant in comparison, and she couldn't help the terror trembling through her as she darted behind an empty pot to hide from the potential danger he posed.

"I've never seen one without wings," he mused. And then he gave his daughter a stern look. "You didn't tear them off, did you?"

"No, Papa! I've been careful with her. I swear it."

Finally, he sighed, relenting against his daughter's request. "You can keep the pixie. But I expect you to take good care of her."

"I will. I promise!"

When the man left, Priscilla turned back to her with a large smile stretched across her face. "Would you like to have a tea party?"

Fatigue still rested on Briar's shoulders, but she tried to shrug it off as she forced a smile. The only tea party she had attended was one she'd secretly watched between several little girls and their dolls. But… "A tea party sounds lovely."

CHAPTER THREE

THE FLARES HAD GIVEN up long ago. But as long as the bonding mark remained on his skin, Quinn refused to give up the search.

He rubbed the green design stretching around his forearm, feeling a tug to Briar. A pull that was unmistakable. She was out there. She was still alive. And as long as she still breathed…

He needed her.

Now more than ever.

With a cautious hand, he reached out to the barrier surrounding their grove, the very thing that hid them from the outside world and protected them from potential predators. As far as prey went, pixies were high on the list of delicious snacks for animals and other magical creatures alike. And if the barrier fell…

His people, the Shades, and the Flare pixies would not last long.

The purple, shimmering barrier rippled and broke in several places like a leaf shredded from the long journey across the kingdom during autumn. Weakness plagued him as he reached for the magic deep within his core and mended the cracks and breaks.

But there were too many. After nineteen long years of holding up the barrier by himself, he was no longer strong enough to keep his people safe.

Heavy footsteps on the other side of the barrier hushed all the pixies within the vicinity, especially his nearby sentries as they slowly and quietly drew swords, bows, and spears. Quinn hardly dared to breathe when a single goblin stepped into view, towering high above him. His green skin formed over muscled arms as he carried an ax over his shoulder. Piercings covered the goblin's face from his nose to his lips to his ears. Leather armor stretched across his muscled torso.

The goblin stopped several paces away and sniffed the air. The violent, bloodthirsty creature would kill them all if he managed to find them, leaving not even a single survivor. The magical barrier hid them from view and disguised their scents. But if it fell…

Perspiration beaded Quinn's forehead as he worked his magic slowly to repair the broken cracks in the protective barrier. In battle, pixies stood little chance against a goblin. And they usually traveled in pairs.

Therefore, he gave every bit of magic he possessed, every speck of energy.

Purple magic flitted through his hand and down his fingertips, joining with the barrier to strengthen it, to keep them invisible to those on the outside. The strain knocked him onto one knee, but he refused to drop his hands and stop the flow of his magic.

He gritted his teeth, fighting against the exhaustion of his duties as the Shade King. He couldn't do this anymore. It was impossible.

I must!

Bonds between souls were nearly unbreakable. He and Briar were bonded, inseparable, each one side of the same coin. The only way he could take a different mate and share his burdens was if Briar died or if she willingly gave up her powers during a special ceremony.

But the bond mark told him she was very much alive.

If he only knew where she was…

Then he wouldn't currently be facing off against a goblin. It must have caught a whiff of their scent.

The goblin took a single step forward, lifting its nose in the air again and sniffing as if trying to relocate their scent. It grasped onto the handle of its ax, ready to strike. A single blow against the barrier likely wouldn't bring it down. But a goblin of all things would not abate when its hunting instincts took over.

Please, he begged, his magic working quickly to repair and strengthen. *Turn away.*

After several long moments, the goblin frowned as it dropped its hand to its side and ambled away in the opposite direction until it disappeared into the forest.

Quinn gasped against the terrible strain, and finally, his magic flickered out when his strength evaded him. His hands dropped onto the ground, bracing him against the soft green and flowering foliage littering the forest floor. Heavy breaths escaped his lungs. His body threatened to collapse. He had no more magic. Nothing left to give. Little by little, it had regenerated slowly without his other half to keep him balanced. But now, it refused to regenerate at all.

The sentries around him released a collective sigh, but if only they knew… Quinn no longer possessed the ability to protect them. Without his magic…

They were all in danger.

"Sire," Matthias, his second in command, said behind him. "The Firewillows are ready for an audience."

Slowly, Quinn's shaky arms pushed him to his feet, and he turned to find the older Flare who had saved his life all those years ago, a white-haired and tan-skinned pixie standing in front of other sentries, awaiting his next orders. The man's gaze darted toward Quinn's tattered wing, and pity briefly flashed across his eyes before his expression became an unreadable mask once more.

Quinn's lips pressed together as he reached for his black cloak and swung it over his shoulders, tying it at the neck to hide his maimed wing.

The assassins hadn't shown their faces again in nearly twenty years, which meant they'd accomplished their goal. Someone out there didn't want Quinn and Briar to bond. They'd unsuccessfully tried to end his line. But it seemed as if Briar's absence appeased whoever was behind his father's murder.

He feared what might happen should they find Briar. He also feared what might happen if they didn't.

His sentries followed behind at a distance, walking rather than flying down the path leading to Mapleborough to "show their respect" to their king. Quinn had insisted at least a thousand times that they could and *should* fly in his presence, even when he couldn't fly himself. But he was too exhausted to berate them now.

At the border, King Florian and Queen Ophelia waited with their own guards, remaining on their side of the line and not daring to cross. Contentions had risen between their two kingdoms over the years. The only reason things hadn't escalated into something more serious was because the Flares relied on his magic to keep their people safe. It was the only advantage he had over them.

Behind him, his sentries remained at a distance as he approached the other two monarchs alone. Each had lighter, pinker skin and lighter hair ranging from brown to blonde.

"We've felt a shift in the atmosphere," King Florian said by way of greeting. "The barrier is weak."

"Because half of the magic is gone," Quinn pointed out, trying to keep the spite out of his voice. "I've been doing my best alone."

"It's not enough anymore."

He clenched his fists at his side, trying to remind himself it wasn't his fault. But the attack felt personal, nonetheless. He tried to cool his anger, but it ended up heating until it burned beneath his skin. He was exhausted and terrified for his people.

"We *need* to find Briar." He hit his fist against the palm of his hand. "We are out of options."

The other king's face reddened as he pointed a finger at him. "Our daughter is gone. There is no hope. Stop breaking our hearts over something that cannot change."

"We need the sun and the moon to protect our people! Without her, we will all perish."

"Then maybe you should die!" the man hissed. "To pass the power to someone else."

The queen patted her husband on the arm. "I know you are frustrated, but we don't truly want him to sacrifice himself. Right, dear?"

When frustration vexed him as well, Quinn threw his arms into the air. "Don't you think I've thought of that? Who would the power pass to? I have no brothers. No heir. I am the only one who can hold this power." He lowered his voice to a dangerous level, barely restraining his anger. "I would die a hundred times over for our people. But I cannot. I need Briar."

"She. Is. Gone!" the other man thundered, and the queen flinched. "We have searched the entire kingdom of Eliandor and well beyond its borders."

"You stopped searching after a year!" Quinn cried, his anger escaping, and he was no longer able to rein it in. "I have sent sentries out *daily* for nineteen years."

"And what fruits do you have to show for your efforts? Nineteen years' worth of resources, wasted!"

"There is no such thing as waste when it comes to the protection of *our* people." Quinn's anger deflated into somberness at being reminded of his failures. He took a moment to steady his breaths as he glanced up at the towering trees high above them. The woodsy scent of bark and wetted leaves wafted off the forest foliage, providing a balm to his restless spirit.

"Why does it have to be you?" the king lamented. "If only my son…"

The Flares hated relying on the Shades for protection. Though, it helped when half of the protection would come from one of their own.

But they both knew Flares could not inherit the power he wielded because they did not have wings. They did not have the power of the moon. Only the power of the sun could complement the moon and make it shine brighter. Not the other way around.

"Perhaps…" Quinn scrubbed an exhausted hand down his face. "My sister Cassie and your son Gabriel… The power of my ancestors has only been passed from male to male down the generations. But if there was no other option… I wonder if it could pass to my sister. And Gabriel could be her equal."

This time, the queen shook her head. "We cannot risk it. You are able to wield it. We know it for sure. We cannot lose what we *do* have based on speculation alone. Throwing away your life is not an option."

A part of him sighed in relief, though he tried not to show it.

"Unless…" The Flare king stroked his beard thoughtfully. "I know we have exhausted all our resources trying to find a way to break this connection between you and Briar so you might take another as your mate. But perhaps there is a stone we have not yet overturned."

Quinn said nothing. Each of them knew the bond could not be broken by anything other than death or a special ceremony with both present. Their situation was precarious.

He tried to offer an alternate solution. "Perhaps if we send out just one more search party—"

"We are done looking for her, Your Highness." King Florian sighed. "Our only option now is to move our people out of the sacred forest and find another home. A safer home. One where we don't need ancient magic to protect us."

"Our flowers will die." Quinn reached across the border to snatch the other man's wrist and held on tight. "They won't survive the trip. And those who do… Is the sacrifice truly worth it? We are safer here than relocating."

King Florian jerked his arm away. "We made our decision already. We are not seeking your permission. We are informing you that we are leaving."

Anger boiled in Quinn's blood at the man's foolishness. Could he not see they were safer here than anywhere else? Leaving meant subjecting his people to death. Besides, this land was sacred to their people. They couldn't just leave. "When?" he ground out through a clenched jaw.

"The end of the week. You may accompany us if you wish. But we are not going to wait for you."

Straightening his cloak, Florian and his wife joined their guards and mounted their mice before spurring the creatures in the opposite direction. Within moments, everyone had disappeared, the only sign that they'd been there were the mice tracks and boot prints on the flattened forest floor.

Quinn returned to Matthias with a scathing glare directed at nothing and everything at once. Aunt Tamara watched with a careful expression where she stood beside his sister, Cassie. His sister took a single step forward, and the area around them hushed as she spoke.

"You are resourceful, Quinn. You must find her. And fast."

"Sire, I advise against looking for her," Matthias said, not for the first time, an intense look in his eye. "You have been too focused on her to the point of obsession. Let nature run its course with her. You must look after your people."

"I am!" he hissed through his teeth. "Without Briar, my magic will deplete until there is nothing left to use to protect our people." Unfortunately, his magic was already gone. He couldn't expend a single drop more.

The man lowered his voice. "A reign without magic could be beneficial. Take a new bride. Have an heir with someone who is not your fated bondmate. And allow the magic to disappear."

Heated anger flashed through his body at the suggestion. "To lose my magic means we will lose our sacred forest. We will have to relocate to safer woods." He glanced over his shoulder at the dozens of guards behind him. Men who had wives and children. *Families.* "But I can't just uproot our people. These sacred lands mean something to us all."

"But sire—"

"We haven't a choice."

He understood Matthias's hesitation with magic. His entire family had been killed by magic in an accident many years ago during his father's reign. The incident had been terribly unfortunate, but all anyone could do was move forward.

And as such, he needed to as well. Everyone seemed to have differing opinions on the action he should take regarding Briar. But he decided to follow the action that felt right in his heart. "Send every sentry we have." If the Flares wouldn't help him, then he must do it alone. "We will find Briar by sundown tomorrow if it's the last thing we do."

CHAPTER FOUR

THE LETHARGY ONLY seemed to worsen over the days since Briar had found a new home with Priscilla. Her body felt abnormally fatigued. Her mind couldn't think straight. No matter how much water she consumed, she always felt thirsty.

She kept telling herself she only needed to adjust to her new home. Beside the river, the air was more humid and less dry. It was much noisier while the house was loud in a *different* way. Chickens clucked below the window she sat beside. A cow lowed somewhere in the distance. The farmer tilled the land, the plow scraping through dirt and rocks in the field.

A bird flitted its wings several times as it passed the house overhead, and not for the first time in the days since her arrival, she found herself searching the skies for pixies. Several dragonflies had drawn her attention. A few butterflies. But otherwise, she hadn't spotted a single pixie.

She wasn't sure what to do if she found one, either.

A cough escaped her lungs when dry dust kicked up from the ground below, forcing her to abandon her place beside the open window.

With bare feet, she climbed down from the ledge, ambled across the slick wood of the table, and sought refuge within her little cottage.

But the somber pit in her stomach only managed to grow larger when her gaze landed on the male pixie Priscilla had cut out of the parchment for her. He now leaned against the wall in her cottage, providing a sense of companionship in a world of immense solitude.

Rather than dwelling on the ever-growing pit, she curtsied to him, imagining they stood in a grand ballroom and he'd asked for her hand in a dance.

"I would love to." She offered her hand, batting her eyelashes at him and pretending he reached for her and pulled her closer.

The eye color of the drawing was muddy, so she couldn't tell if they were brown, green, purple, or blue. But his black hair matched the color of his outfit. His wings were a purple hue. And she liked to imagine that he was handsome.

Briar hummed to herself as she gently took each of the pixie's paper hands and twirled with him around the cottage. Together, they danced and spun and floated as if on air. A gentle hand on her waist. A light touch to her fingers. And in her mind, he gazed at her with loving eyes.

All too suddenly, the daydream popped when his paper head flopped backward, breaking the illusion that he was real.

An aching pit of loneliness crawled through her chest as she held his limp form in her arms. He wasn't real. But she so desperately wanted him to be. Although she was content enough living with Priscilla...

She was lonely.

Pixies were out there somewhere. She didn't know where. But she wanted to join them, to become a part of their world, to return home. Wherever that home was.

She blinked back heavy tears filled with heartache, trying her best to keep her emotions from spilling out. As long as her flower remained here, she was good and stuck. How could she find other pixies if she couldn't even leave the house?

Pounding footsteps climbed the stairs. Briar swiftly wiped her eyes and leaned the parchment pixie back against the wall. She cleared her throat and managed a smile as she exited the cottage in time for Priscilla to enter the room.

"We're going to the city!" The girl spun in a circle and twirled her skirts. "Time to pack up! I'm going to take you—"

"Leave the pixie," her father grumbled from downstairs, loud enough for her to hear his voice. "The city is no place for someone like her."

"Aww," the girl whined. "Why can't she come with us?"

"Because she can't. Leave some food out. She'll be just fine on her own for a little while."

Whispering, the girl said, "Maybe you can hide in my pocket—"

"Priscilla," her father warned. "Leave her. We're going. Now."

The girl pouted as she packed a portmanteau with several dresses and other items of clothing. Uneasiness twisted her stomach when she noticed more than one dress going with her.

"How long will you be gone?"

"Papa said a week or two." She sniffed and wiped her eyes. "We're visiting my aunt in the city about an inheritance. Papa won't let me stay home."

When Priscilla moved near enough, Briar touched her large hand reassuringly. "You will have a wonderful time. I just know it."

With a smile, the girl patted the top of Briar's head with a finger. It was all she could do to remain on her feet rather than allowing her legs to collapse beneath her from the weight. "Oh, I do wish I could embrace you."

And then Priscilla unlatched the window but stuffed a short stick beneath, so it remained open just enough for

Briar to slip beneath if needed. "Don't want any birds snatching you while I'm gone." She spun around, grabbed her things, and set out a small bundle of food and water on the table before she gave her one final wave and disappeared.

Within minutes, Briar made out the sounds of a horse being hitched to a wagon and then clomping hooves as they traveled down the path leading away from the property and toward the supposed city.

A dry raspiness clung to Briar's throat. Unable to hold herself up any longer when the fatigue drained all energy from her body, she slumped against the outside wall of her cottage and closed her eyes for a few moments.

What was the matter with her? She didn't feel sick. Just extremely fatigued and thirsty. It wasn't normal for her. It was as if the life was slowly draining out of her, and no matter what she tried, she couldn't reverse it.

Her eyes snapped wide open in alarm when she finally realized what was happening.

She struggled to her feet, tipping one way and then the other when remaining upright proved difficult. With stumbling steps, she rushed toward the window, placing her hands against the glass as she glanced down below at the garden.

Outside, the goldenblush briar was tangled in weeds, suffocating and fighting for air in dry soil. Icy dread fell over her.

"Hold on!" she said to her flower as she moved away from the window and glanced around for something her size that she might be able to use to water the bloom.

She spotted a bucket sitting beside her cottage, and her heart soared. She grabbed a hold of the handle, but it was stuck to the side of the cottage as if it were glued. She frowned. After several tugs, the bucket unlatched from the side, and she rushed toward the window once more.

But before she managed to reach it, the stick holding it upright snapped.

And the window slid closed.

"No!" She dropped her bucket and tried in vain to lift the window with her own two hands. But no matter how hard she pried and pulled, pushed and lifted, it refused to budge.

Her flower was dying in the garden.

And she was trapped inside.

What was she supposed to do?

CHAPTER FIVE

QUINN HISSED AS THE leafy brand on his arm burned.

He glanced down at the bonding brand. The green markings were beginning to fade on his skin, starting from one end of the brand toward the other. He swallowed the lump in his throat.

It was disappearing. Briar was dying.

"Caw!" The crow he rode on exclaimed its distress as if echoing the panicked turmoil running rampant through his own body.

Wind whipped through his hair as he more frantically searched the ground below. The bird swooped downward through tangled trees and high grasses, spiraled upward toward the clouds, and swooped once more. His knuckles turned white from clenching onto the bird's bridle to prevent himself from falling. But when Briar's life was in danger, he refused to cease his efforts.

When their search moved from swampland to cornfields, he ordered his men to branch outward to cover as much ground as possible. Fear wavered in his eyes as he glanced down at his brand once more. It was still fading. Halfway gone now.

They wouldn't find her in time. He knew that. It was a vain hope. But he refused to give up. As long as she still lived, there was always hope.

Tinkling wind chimes pulled his attention toward the farmhouse in the distance, and for a moment, he hesitated. Humans were dangerous for pixies. Their curiosity and desire to study them had already killed more of them than he could count, resulting in broken wings and tragic deaths.

As the brand continued to fade, he gritted his teeth. He turned his crow in the direction of the house, the dark creature flapping its wings and soaring smoothly through the skies.

With a gesture of his hand, Quinn signaled to Matthias and another pixie to accompany him to the house.

"Sire!" Matthias shouted over the winds, nodding his head in the opposite direction. "It's not likely that she's in human lands. We must continue our search elsewhere."

Quinn's eyebrows drew together as he glanced at the fading brand once again. Once upon a time, he had felt a strong tug through the bond when it had urged him to save Briar's seed from falling to its death. He felt a similar tug now. She was close.

"We have to try, anyway."

The Flare pixie sidled his own swallow up to follow him on one side while the Shade flew on the other. Like him, Matthias couldn't fly and relied on a bird for transportation.

"Search the property!" he called over the high winds rushing at his face. "I gauge we have less than an hour to find her before she's lost to us!"

When they reached the farmhouse, the three of them branched off in different directions, searching the ground for a golden flower. Quinn was sure they had already searched this area of Eliandor, but he couldn't explain it… If she was anywhere, he felt as if she would be here.

He rounded the house and flew over the river, frowning when the high grasses made it impossible to spot any sort of hidden foliage or flower. He would have to walk on foot to search. But there was so much area to cover that he didn't know where to start.

Rather than dismounting, he pulled up on the reins and guided the crow higher into the sky, planning to search the river as a last resort.

"Sire!" the Shade sentry bellowed.

Quinn turned his head sharply toward the man, and his heart jolted in shock to find him circling fast around a section of the garden, the fast wings cutting quickly through the air and ruffling the flowers below from the movement.

He circled around a goldenblush briar.

He urged the crow closer, and before the bird even touched the ground, Quinn leaped off and stumbled toward the golden bloom.

Vines wrapped around the stem, stealing its water from the ground and blocking off its sunlight. Several golden petals littered the dirt floor at the base of the flower, and Quinn stooped low, running a hand over one of the petals to find it brittle and dry. Around the base of the flower, the dirt churned white. Although he dared not touch the white substance, he recognized it as a poison of pixiemake.

A linear mark at the base of the stem suggested a small blade must have tried to cut the strong stalk without success before the attempted murderer tried other methods such as poison and strangling. His gaze snapped up to find the rest of the petals wilting, ready to drop with the next gale or rainfall. It was dying. Which was likely the reason Briar was, too.

No pixie ever ventured far from their flower. She was close by.

"Free the flower from the vines!" he shouted loud enough for other pixies in the area to hear him and come rushing his way. "Dig it up. Keep the roots intact. Be mindful of the poison."

He gritted his teeth when he realized transporting the flower back home would be an impossible feat. They weren't prepared to move it on such short notice. The only thing large enough to accomplish the feat…

Was his crow.

Quinn would have to do it. No one else could command the bird quite as carefully.

His stomach twisted at the thought of allowing anyone else but himself to handle Briar. Especially when a pixie had already tried to kill her. But there was no choice in the matter.

With a single swoop of his leg, he mounted his crow and took to the skies once more, now searching for a Flare with green eyes. He knew nothing else about Briar. What color her hair was. How tall she was. What she dressed in. But he hoped he would know her when he saw her.

He circled the property as fast as his crow allowed him, dodging between trees, searching around stacks of hay, and as he gained more courage, he looped several times around the house.

Thankfully, he didn't spot any humans nearby, only horses and other livestock.

Please, he begged whatever magic bonded him to Briar. *Please let me find her.*

Almost as soon as he voiced the plea in his head, he spotted a shimmer of gold out of the corner of his eye. He turned his crow around, searching once more for the gold. It flashed briefly again, coming from one of the windows on the property.

With a quiet flap of its wings, the crow landed on top of the window ledge. Again, Quinn dismounted, wary of the small ledge and the steep drop that could lead to his death. He cupped his hands around his eyes and peered through the glass of the window. His gaze passed over a bed with a canopy hanging over it, pictures tacked to the walls, and then his attention landed on the small cottage sitting on top of one of the tables, just large enough for a pixie—

He gasped when he noticed the pixie-sized, womanly figure lying on her side with long, golden hair cascading over her face and shoulders. Her chest rose and fell with each slow breath. But she wasn't just asleep. She was dying.

With one forceful shove to the window, he discovered it was good and shut, too difficult for one pixie to open by his lonesome.

As if his men were watching him, he gestured for help with his hand, and they came flying. A team of them lifted from the top of the window, opening it just a crack. He dove through the crack moments before the window shut behind him once more.

Quinn rushed to the woman's side, and his heart caught in his throat as he turned her onto her back. The golden of her hair shimmered just like the petals on the goldenblush briar. And when it fell to the side to reveal her face…

Warm awe filled the cavern of his chest as his gaze flitted over her beautiful features. The soft curve of her jaw. The heart shape of her face. The sweet plumpness of her lips.

He barely managed to tear his gaze away long enough to glance at her arm. The violet bonding brand confirmed her identity.

Briar Firewillow.

And then his heart gave another start when he spotted the drawing of a pixie she lay beside. Purple skin. Black hair. Purple wings.

It looked like…

Him.

Knowing time was scarce, he rolled up the drawing and tucked it beneath his cloak before scooping Briar into his arms. She felt lighter than she should, almost as if she had barely managed to survive in the years of her absence.

The pixies at the window lifted it once more upon his approach, higher this time, which allowed him to duck beneath it with Briar in his arms. The window crashed closed behind him. But he didn't look back. He kept his gaze forward.

"Matthias!" he ordered in a commanding tone, and his second in command mounted his swallow and flew up to the ledge. He carefully handed Briar to him. There was no one else he trusted more. "Get her home as fast as your swallow can carry you. Take half the guards with you."

The more people who surrounded Briar, the safer she would be from the threat of harm.

The man seemed to come to the same conclusion as he had. "She won't make it, sire."

"She *has* to!" He momentarily squeezed his eyes shut as the next order physically pained him. He didn't want to do it this way. But they had no choice and so little time. "Get her home and marry her to me by proxy. The marriage bond will lend her my life force and prepare her to accept her half of the magic."

The first ceremony when they were children had bonded them together. The marriage ceremony, and then touching his bare skin for the first time, would activate her magic. And the final ceremony to take up her mantle over their people would bind them and their magic together until death.

Instead of questioning his decision, Matthias nodded before spurring his mount into the air and darting in the direction of home with half the sentries accompanying him.

The other half helped dig out and lift Briar's flower, and after Quinn mounted his crow, they jumped down from the window ledge. The pixies lifted the flower higher until the bird grasped onto it with its feet. They would have to fly slowly to protect it from the wind.

And to shield it even further, a cluster of pixies flew directly ahead of him to block the wind from reaching the flower's petals. They would arrive home far later than

Briar. But lending his life force to her would give her more time.

Please survive, he silently begged as he stared down at the bonding brand, which seemed to be fading faster by the minute. *I need you. I can't do this without you.*

And so, he dared to hope. Because hope was the only thing he could hold onto.

CHAPTER SIX

EVERYTHING HURT.

Excruciating pain shot down Briar's spine as she blinked her eyes open and tried to sit up. But her body refused to obey her. Darkness clouded the edges of her vision, making it impossible to understand where she was.

A dozen different faces shifted in and out of her line of sight before moving into the darkness once more. She couldn't tell how far away they were. Likely far because their faces were small like a human's when they were across the room. But somehow... They seemed so close. As if they were her own size.

She opened her mouth to speak, but like her body, her tongue refused to obey her. Darkness closed in on her again. She fought with all her might to swim to lighter waters. And she managed it just long enough to see an older man with white hair standing above her.

"—bind you in marriage to King Quinn Thistlethorn." Muffled voices followed, and then… "—as proxy, I accept your hand in marriage. Do you accept your king?"

A spurt of hot panic shot through her. But her head was woozy, and her vision unclear. Where was she? Who were these people? She did not want to marry anyone.

Briar coughed weakly as she tried to push the older man away, but her body proved too weak. "No," she rasped.

A woman dressed in lavish black and gold clothing stood over her, black hair pinned up in a bun, and the few wrinkles on her purple-gray face revealing her older age. But it wasn't her skin that gave her pause. It was her *wings*.

A pixie. Just like her.

"Darling," the woman murmured as she sat on the edge of the bed beside her and smoothed her hair back like a mother would. "My name is Tamara. You are safe now. But you are dying. We must bond you in marriage to the king. If we don't, you will not make it."

Briar weakly lifted her hand and grasped the woman's wrist. It was small. Like hers.

Hot tears trailed from the corners of her eyes and down her face. These people were pixies. After so long…she was finally home.

"Do you, Briar Firewillow, accept Quinn Thistlethorn's hand in marriage?" the voice asked again somewhere behind her. But her head refused to turn when it felt so stiff and achy.

She felt it. A weakness in her body. Her flower was dying. And soon, it would succumb altogether and drag her down with it. The only choice she had was to trust these pixies. To hope they would not lead her astray. To save her...

She could not do this alone any longer. She desperately needed help, even if this wasn't the path she would have chosen for herself.

Squeezing her eyes shut, several more tears escaped. She had no choice but to marry the old man with the white hair. It was either marry him or die. And she did not want to die. Not now when she was so close to learning who she was.

"I do," she said, choking on another sob.

She didn't remember the rest because the darkness dragged her back under the surface of hazy waters, and everything became foggy and black.

Quinn cried out in alarm, clutching his chest when a sudden, intense fatigue stole the life and energy from his body. His head swam with darkness. His world tipped upside down. And when his mind spun too much to keep himself upright, his grip on the crow's feathers slackened, and his body became limp as he slipped off the flying creature.

Wind whipped through his hair. His cloak fluttered in a fast breeze. He saw the faintest glimpse of silver stars sparkling in the night sky before someone slipped their arms beneath his shoulders and caught him in the air. They swooped low to the ground with the momentum, long blades of grass brushing against his boots.

And then they darted into the skies once more, away from the unforgiving death of crashing to the ground.

"Hold on, Your Highness," the sentry said as he adjusted his grip on him. He wrapped one of Quinn's arms around his shoulders and another sentry took the other. "We're almost home."

Quinn sighed with exhaustion, allowing his body to slump when his energy had been halfway drained. But he was far from upset. Rather, he was overcome by *relief*. Briar had accepted him. She would live long enough for them to try to save her flower.

He barely managed to crack his eyes open to find that one of the sentries now rode the crow, steering him back toward home when Quinn was no longer able to do it himself. The man struggled with controlling the animal, but they were close enough to home that it didn't matter a great deal, as the bird knew where to go.

They soared over the trees, the moonlight reflecting off their leafy boughs. And when they entered the heart of the forest, they descended beneath the branches and flew straight through the barrier that blocked out anything other than a pixie.

Mapleborough lay in the distance on their right and Shadowfalls on their left.

The crisp scent of earthy bark and fresh water greeted him as they darted over a lake bustling with Shades as they flew, fished for tadpoles, or conversed beside the water. Many homes had been built near the water, or in some cases, floated on top. And as they delved into a woodsier area, the boughs were teeming with activity. Pixies worked or played, many stopping their activities to stare at him with curious concern.

But they didn't stop. Because they couldn't. Not when Briar's flower needed care.

Half the sentries branched off in another direction while the other half accompanied him to his land. A small pond was shaded by numerous plants, flowers, and trees, creating a private and secluded setting from the rest of the forest. Pixie houses resided around the pond, all connected by one long, wooden path suspended above the water to prevent it from getting wet.

His aunt's house was on the left side of the pond, his sister's on the right. Several more important people also owned houses in this area, including Matthias. The pixie palace, his own home, was at the farthest end of the pond, larger than the others, with a couple connecting homes to house servants or guests.

They flew past the palace and into the nearby grove where his moonshade flower resided, opening its purple petals and basking in the moonlight. The area received enough moonlight *and* sunlight for both their flowers to thrive.

Without preamble, the sentries began digging a new hole near his flower, and despite his lack of strength, Quinn insisted on helping. Fatigue burned through his body, and more than anything, he wanted to collapse and sleep for an entire week.

But he dug deep enough into fertile soil for the goldenblush briar's roots to reach. Together, they lowered the flower into the ground and tucked more soil around its base before giving it the antidote to the pixie poison. The flower drooped, threatening to break off its own stem and shed its remaining petals. They supported it by tying it to a sturdy stick and filled buckets from the pond to water the flower down to its roots.

They worked almost tirelessly to save the flower, and not once did Quinn leave its side, even as the dawn stretched over the sky, which then led into yet another dusk. He counted two more tiresome dusks before the goldenblush briar at last accepted the soil and dug its roots deeper into the ground. The stem became sturdier, and new petals began to grow. Only then did Quinn collapse on the ground beside the flower and succumb to sleep with guards to watch over him.

It wasn't long before someone shook him awake. Through bleary eyes, he recognized Matthias's face hovering above him, the white of his hair standing out against the tanned tone of his skin.

He sat up in alarm as he took in his second in command as well as the half-dozen guards surrounding him. "What happened? Is Briar lost to us?"

As he glanced up at the flower he still lay beneath, he noticed a happy bloom. Briar was still alive, and she was thriving.

Matthias shook his head and gestured toward the palace. "She's beginning to stir. Might I suggest you get cleaned up, Your Highness? Perhaps making a favorable impression would be best for your first meeting."

He grimaced at the dirt marring his clothing and skin. His hair was a mess, strands sticking up all over his head. And he reckoned the slight stench might have been him, as he hadn't bathed nor changed his clothes in, well, several days.

One of the servants drew him a hot bath in his room, and he rushed to scrub the dirt from his skin and clean-shaven face and washed his shoulder-length black hair. Choosing an outfit proved to be difficult when he wanted to make the most favorable impression on Briar but didn't want to appear too *kingly*. He settled on a slim black outfit made for sparring and riding rather than attending kingly meetings or doing other kingly duties.

The black leather, sleeveless vest drew attention to the muscles in his arms, but after a moment of hesitancy, he shrugged on a long, leather coat to hide his broken wing beneath it. His black leather trousers tucked into black boots, and then as he faced the mirror…

Self-consciousness shivered down his spine.

Was it too much black? Would she look at him in disgust if she learned of his wing? Was his appearance not what she preferred? What if she didn't like the look of a Shade and preferred a Flare instead?

He held his hands out in front of him and stared down at the purple-gray tint of his skin and the long black fingernails extending from his fingers to sharp points. He'd become the Shade King at the age of six. He'd blundered through learning his magic when no one had ever given him the proper instruction. He'd led his people alone, even though some of his decisions had been poor and reckless, and now he must protect Briar to the best of his ability when he no longer knew who he could trust.

But never until this day had he felt so…inadequate.

His *wife* rested in the other room. She hadn't even seen him before agreeing to marry him. She didn't know what he looked like, his temperament, nor the workings of his heart and soul. And to be fair, he didn't know hers, either.

Could they make this marriage work? Or was it doomed for failure?

Quinn nervously smoothed his clothing and fixed his hair before he crossed the length of his room, placed his hand on the door handle, and took a deep breath.

It was time to meet his wife.

CHAPTER SEVEN

BRIAR GROANED, STRETCHING her aching muscles as she woke from a deep slumber. Her previously spinning head had calmed, and her limbs didn't feel quite so heavy as they had before she'd fallen into the cool waters of unconsciousness.

Slowly, she blinked her eyes open, squinting against the light emanating from purple orbs in black metal sconces attached to the walls of...

Well, she didn't know where she was.

It wasn't the cottage she had previously occupied in Priscilla's home. But rather, everything *belonged*. Nothing seemed out of place as if it had been carved out of a piece of wood mainly for decoration.

She pushed herself into a sitting position as her gaze dragged along the bookcases filled with dozens of books with beautiful leather bindings, all her very own size. The tables and chairs were masterfully crafted with elegant, swirling designs giving life to the inanimate objects. She lay on top of a bed with a soft white duvet, the headboard crafted of swirling metal designs similar to the other furniture in the room.

And when she swiveled her legs over the side of the bed, the new vantage point gave her a view of the several small plants shooting out of porcelain pots. Her paper pixie peered at her from beside one of the plants, leaning against the wall with its familiar black and purple colors, and a smile lifted on her face. The parchment was slightly crinkled, and one of his arms curled in a funny position.

"Um…hello."

Briar screamed from being startled, and unable to catch herself in time, she fell off the bed and landed with a *thump* on the floor. She scrambled to her feet and spun around, backing up against the wall opposite from the direction she'd heard the voice.

Each breath escaped as quick spurts of air as her gaze honed in on a man with straight black hair to his shoulders, the top half of his hair tied behind his head to reveal his pointed ears. His skin was a purple-gray hue, and he wore all black from his clothing to the coat around his shoulders.

Black eyebrows lifted as he also seemed to take her in, one corner of his dark gray lips quirking up on one side. And his eyes… Violet in color. Full of curiosity and levity.

The breath fled from her as she gazed into the beautiful hue of those eyes. He looked just like her parchment pixie come to life. Tall with broad shoulders and a handsome face. The only thing he didn't appear to have were wings. That's where he differed from her pixie.

He lifted a finger, the tip of his black nail tapping against his bottom lip. "I apologize for frightening you. I came up with several different greetings over the past few hours, and the one I ended up using sounded more awkward than I intended." He chuckled and fixed his violet stare on her. "What more could I have said in this situation? I'm glad to finally meet you? I'm glad we are reunited? Thank you for not dying? You see, I'm not exactly sure *what* to say."

"Who are you?" she asked, her voice trembling.

"Someone who has been searching for you for a long time...*Briar Firewillow*."

"How do you know my name?" She backed up further until her fingers brushed against one of the spines of the books. As a weapon, it wouldn't do her much good. But he didn't stop her from taking it and holding it against her chest, waiting to smack him with it if necessary.

The man ran a hand over his mouth from where he leaned against the farthest wall, his ankles crossed in a casual manner. "It's a rather long story. Do you care to sit for a tale?"

She didn't sit. But she didn't order him to leave, either. Because she wanted to hear his tale. She wanted to know the truth.

Finally, she nodded.

He poured a steaming cup of tea and placed it on a table between them, though he moved no closer. Rather, he leaned against the wall, crossed his arms, and stared down at his feet. Who was he? A servant? She knew nothing of this culture, but who else would serve her tea other than a servant in a lavish room such as this?

"When you were just a small seed, you were bonded to the prince of the Shades. Little Princess Briar Firewillow. Unfortunately, your seed was stolen and lost, and we only found you recently."

Her voice trembled. "That's not such a long story."

He shrugged, half of his mouth upturned in a grin. "It would be if I were a good storyteller. I am rather terrible with details."

The information overwhelmed her, and it created a pit of heartache in her chest when she realized how much she must have missed out on. What seemed like only yesterday, she'd simply been lonely little Briar who didn't know she was a pixie.

And today?

If what the pixie said was true, she was a pixie princess. Now married to the Shade King.

She recalled brief glimpses of the king. Tan skin. White, curly hair. Old.

And unable to help herself, sobs burst from her mouth and tears trailed down her face. Oh, how had she landed from one unfortunate situation to another? True, she was alive and well. On the mend. But now she was trapped in a marriage she didn't want.

"Why are you crying?" the pixie asked softly.

She hiccupped and wiped her eyes. "I'm married to an old man."

His eyebrows shot up. "What? You thought… Oh." And then his lips twitched as if he found her predicament amusing. He uncrossed his arms and leveled her with a pitying stare. "He must be terrible."

"He must be absolutely horrid," she sniffed.

"And putridly ugly."

"Oh no," she lamented, wiping her eyes again but the tears kept coming.

"And older than a bag of dusty bones."

Briar sobbed harder, hiding her face in her hands. She was alive and well, yes. But did this truly have to be the price for her life? To be married to an old stranger? One who had not bothered to come visit her in her recovery?

Although the worst of her tears began to subside, she still dabbed her eyes with the hem of her sleeve. "Why did this have to happen to me?" Her vision cleared enough for her to view the pixie with a little less than a blur. "Tell me, pixie servant. How can I escape this situation?"

He tapped his fingers on his lips as if deep in thought. "Perhaps you ought to give the poor man a chance. He's dedicated so much of his life to searching for you, after all."

"But to be trapped between marriage and dying? I had no choice in the matter. This was not my choice."

He tipped his head to the side, studying her with his soulful violet eyes. "What would you choose, Briar? I want you to be happy."

She snorted in her misery. "I am glad you want to look after my happiness. But what does your word count for against the word of a king?"

The man grimaced, rubbing the back of his neck with his hand. "Well…you see… I'm not exactly…well…a servant…"

She took in the guardsman uniform he wore and realized she must have incorrectly deduced his station. "A guard," she corrected with a sigh. "I don't understand this culture yet." She gestured to her parchment pixie. "You gave me quite the startle. For a moment, I thought you were my friend come to life. But you don't have wings."

His lips pressed together as he lifted one side of his coat to reveal the purple shimmer of translucent wings, hidden beneath the black material. "I do, in fact, have wings."

"Oh. I apologize." Her hands flew to her cheeks when they burned with heat. "I didn't know."

Someone rapped on the door, startling her into dropping her book to the ground with a *thud*. She scrambled to pick up some of the pages that had come loose and scattered across the ground while the guard strode past her and opened the door.

A man wearing a similar black guardsman uniform stood on the opposite side of the door, and Briar couldn't help but stare. Never in her life had she met small people like herself, so seeing many in such a short time took her aback.

The man also had black hair, though cropped short, with a long, straight nose and light gray eyes.

"Please forgive my disturbance." The man dipped his head. "But I have grave news."

"What is it?" the guard asked with a serious expression burning through his eyes.

"One of the sentries has been found dead."

His expression hardened. "What was it? A predator?"

The other man shook his head. "The wounds are pixiemade. He was killed by one of our own."

Quinn cursed under his breath as he viewed the place where the sentry had been murdered. Vines were flattened where the man's body had lain, and specks of blood still remained on the forest floor.

But the most concerning thing wasn't the blood or the body. It was the threat of more killings in the future.

He rubbed a torn piece of red cloth between his fingers, stabbed through with a knife and lodged into the trunk of a tree directly above where the murder had taken place. For a moment, his mind flashed back to the day it felt as if his soul had died its first death. Nineteen years ago. Flashes of red cloaks. Screams. Blood. A sense of hopelessness.

He knew without a doubt…

They were back.

And it was no coincidence that this happened right as Briar returned home.

"Matthias," Quinn murmured quietly as he approached his second in command, not sure yet if he trusted the other soldiers when he wasn't sure what to think himself. "How long ago did you inform King and Queen Firewillow about Briar's return?"

"Two mornings ago, sire." His expression was hard, his eyes dark and filled with anger, whether at the murder or promise of bloodshed, he didn't know. "Briar is young and experienced. The threat of the Red Cloaks has returned. Goblins scour the land just outside the border. She's not ready for this." He lowered his voice. "Reject her in the upcoming ceremony. The warlock can break your bond only then. And you can choose another."

Quinn bit the inside of his cheek as his gaze drifted back to the red fabric pinned to the tree. It was a warning. No…not a warning. A *promise*. If Briar was alive, someone would try to tear them apart. The danger was close. Imminent. And she knew very little of their people and customs. He saw the truth in Matthias's warning.

But…

He couldn't help but recall the bright green of her eyes, her outward beauty and the beauty of her countenance. The woman was resilient to have survived away from society for so long. She was already incredible, and he knew there was so much more to discover about her.

And…he had to admit, if only to himself, that the moment they'd locked eyes, he'd felt the stirring of hope. A hope for love. He wanted it. More than anything. The thought of throwing her away for another, if only for the sake of his people, left a sour taste in his mouth.

"She's not ready. No one else needs to die," his second in command urged, the man's voice cracking as if recalling the way his family was taken from him. Quinn had been young when the incident had happened, but he could never forget the day his mother had died. The day his people went to war with the Flares.

His muddled thoughts turned back to the day nineteen years ago. Someone had assassinated his father. If Quinn hadn't dived off the balcony, would he have met the same fate? And why hadn't they tried again all these years?

Because Briar had been missing… Half of the power had been gone.

Although he still didn't understand who was behind the attack and only had an inkling of what they wanted to accomplish, he knew one thing only—he needed to protect Briar at all costs.

Shaking his head, he said, "Even someone new would have to learn how to wield the power. Briar deserves a chance. She was bonded to me before she even sprouted. She was born to do this. And I would like to let her try."

Raising his voice to everyone within the vicinity, he said, "I want you to investigate this incident further. Find out who's behind this. And Matthias…" He turned to find the man with his eyebrows drawn, his mouth pinched. "Come with me." Beneath his coat, half of his wings fluttered with antsy anticipation, but the other half refused to obey him. He instead mounted his crow. "I will speak with the Flares and rally our troops. Whatever we are facing… The threat is now on the inside. And we need to be prepared."

Matthias mounted his swallow, and with several guards accompanying them, Quinn and his second in command flew to the border and waited for an audience with the Flare monarchs. Usually, Quinn found this process tedious and frustratingly time-consuming, especially when Florian liked to make him wait if only to watch him squirm. But this time, the monarchs hurried to the border with their own soldiers, only to frown when they glanced from him to Matthias and to the guards behind them. As if they were looking for someone…

Gabriel smirked, the Flare prince crossing his arms as he spoke first. "No Briar? Why am I not surprised? You fabricated this entire story to keep us in the grove."

Quinn gritted his teeth. "It's not fabricated. Briar is resting."

The prince nodded toward him. "Show us then. Let's see proof of your magic to make sure."

Rather than lifting his hand, he clenched his fists at his side. "I can't. She has not yet touched me to bring forth her own magic and complement mine."

Florian and Ophelia glanced dubiously at one another, the light of hope falling from their eyes and quickly replaced by despair.

Matthias took a step forward. "She is real. It's her. I've seen her bonding brand with my own eyes." He and Gabriel made eye contact, and the prince's cool glare appeared right on time.

With a shake of his head, Quinn interrupted the silent battle of wills. "The Red Cloaks killed someone in Shadowfalls. I came to warn you."

A rapid, hushed conversation broke out between the king and queen. Florian shook his head, and Ophelia's expression fell into dejection as she turned away and allowed several soldiers to escort her home.

Florian said, "My wife wants to visit this girl you claim as Briar. But if the Red Cloaks are active again, I will not allow her to cross the border. Bring Briar here. Tomorrow. Otherwise, the Flares will be leaving in two days' time."

"Fair enough."

"Allow me to cross." Gabriel stepped closer until he toed the line of the border between kingdoms. He lowered his voice. "I can confirm Briar's identity, and we can…" His previous smirk returned, though Quinn recognized the underlying uncertainty beneath. "Compare notes on the Red Cloaks, if you will."

Quinn glanced over his shoulder to find Matthias's hard stare on Gabriel, though he likely couldn't have heard what the prince said in hushed tones.

What notes could Gabriel possibly have that Quinn didn't? Allowing the prince over the border would only hinder his progress and slow him down when he needed to track the killer *now*.

Therefore, he shook his head and addressed Gabriel and Florian simultaneously. "I'll bring Briar tomorrow morning. She's still in…shock…after the entire ordeal."

"No games." Florian turned to mount his rodent. "If she's a fake, we'll begin our travels and leave your people behind."

As the others disappeared from sight, Quinn wanted to pull out his hair and shout at the skies in frustration. Too much animosity still lingered between their people. Quinn was suspicious of them, and they were distrustful of him. Briar could mend the gap. She had to!

"Let's go," he ordered his guards. "The killer is still out there, and I refuse to allow them to strike again."

When curiosity trumped her fatigue, Briar finally braved the world outside her room.

She smoothed down her skirts, took a deep breath, and before she could allow herself even a moment's hesitation more, she slipped out the door...

Only to be faced with a series of hallways and rooms filled with unfamiliar styles of decoration. Everything had a woodsy, natural feel to it, and it was as if she'd left her home beside the river and stepped into another.

Smooth floors stretched out in front of her, and as she entered a larger room connecting the many hallways within the palace-like home, she marveled at her surroundings. Orbs danced with purple light in black, curled metal sconces. Several chairs lay in the corner of the room, with dark blue and red cushions tied to more black metal curling in intricate patterns. A staircase curved to an upper floor balcony, which appeared to lead to more hallways or rooms.

Her feet seemed to float on clouds as she found the exit of the palace and stepped outside into the light of dusk. Plenty of guards surrounded the property, who eyed her curiously but said nothing.

All breath fled from her when she found herself staring out over glistening waters reflecting the pink, orange, and yellow hues of a sunset sky with magical, colorful orbs of light dancing across the water. She leaned against the balcony and sighed with a moment of contentment as she watched several pixies dart over the lake with wings glistening black, red, purple, or white.

A woman with short black hair sweeping over her forehead waved frantically with her arms from where she perched on a tree branch hanging over the pond. "Briar!" she called. "Hello! I'm Cassie!"

Briar's face lit up as she leaned over the railing and waved back. "Oh, hello!" She didn't know who the woman was, but she looked remarkably similar to the guard she'd met only hours earlier. Perhaps they were related?

Next to her sat an older woman, delicate and poised with a regal expression on her face, not a single black hair out of place. She'd seen the woman before during the wedding ceremony. Tamara. She, too, looked similar to the guard. Perhaps his mother or an aunt?

"If you are looking for Quinn, he's over by the training fields." Cassie pointed to what likely was a field behind several towering trees.

All at once, a cold dread fell to her toes. Cassie was speaking about Briar's husband. King Quinn Thistlethorn.

The last thing she wanted was to meet her own husband. But she couldn't hide away forever. After all, she owed him her life. The least she could do was properly thank him for his sacrifice.

Hugging her arms closer to her chest to lend her comfort in a foreign world and discomforting situation, she traversed a wooden path that led around the lake with several guards following her. The path branched off to the left down a dirt road leading through a thick copse of trees.

She couldn't help but marvel at how clear the pathways were. No vines or tall grasses were trying to grab her ankles. Not even a fallen branch or leaf blocked the path ahead to make traversing it difficult or impossible altogether.

She wrung her hands as she made out the metal clangs and hisses in the distance, and when she broke out of the trees, her stomach twisted with nerves when she spotted a wide range of soldiers sparring on a large field.

Was the king on the field? Or was he watching from a distance?

Her question was quickly answered as she spotted the man she recognized from her hazy memories leaning against a hitching post. Like her, he didn't have any wings. Wrinkles lay within the folds of his skin. His white hair was a stark contrast to his tan skin tone. And when she approached, he bowed at the waist, his expression stating he'd already known she was there. The sword at his waist swung with the movement of his bow before he addressed her. "Princess."

Princess...

She certainly didn't feel like a princess, and a part of her wasn't sure she believed she was who everyone thought she was.

Briar bowed her head, more from shame than acknowledgement. All her life, she had dreamed of loving and being loved in return. This was not how she had imagined her dreams coming to life. But…

"Forgive me," she murmured, keeping her gaze on her feet rather than looking at him. "A guard told me I should give you and our marriage a chance. I should not have said some of the things I said. Yes, we have a vast difference in age, but perhaps if we just get to know each other…"

She dared to lift her head to find his eyes narrowed as if trying to connect the pieces to a puzzle. "Guard?" The man lifted an eyebrow.

"I think he may have been a guard, at least," she continued with pursed lips. "He wore a guardsman uniform."

And like the guard, now the man's lips lifted as if he found her predicament amusing as well. He pointed a finger to the distant field where a few dozen soldiers stood talking amongst themselves. "He's not in that group, perchance, is he?"

Briar scanned the group, searching for the man in question. Her heart shot to her throat when she spotted him, nearly hidden behind three other soldiers. She found it difficult to find him when he hid his wings while the others flaunted theirs.

"There he is. The one with the black coat."

The king's shoulders shook silently as if he were now laughing at her.

Planting her hands on her hips, she glared at him. "What do you find so funny?" she demanded. "I said I would give you a chance. Why are you laughing at me?"

"I'm not, Your Highness." He coughed into his hand, and his shoulders ceased shaking. Barely. "You were hardly lucid during the marriage ceremony. I can imagine a few…*important* details may have flown your mind." He coughed again and leaned against the railing. "You are mistaking me for someone else, Princess Briar. Indeed, I was at the ceremony. Acting as your king's *proxy*. I am Matthias, second in command. Yours and Quinn's guard." He gestured to the man in the cloak. "And there he is. King Quinn Thistlethorn. Ruler of the Shade kingdom. Your husband."

"My…" Her mouth dried as she looked Quinn over with renewed eyes. But then her entire face heated, and her hands flew to her mouth as she recalled the spectacle she'd made in his presence. Sobbing over the idea of being married to the king. Worried over the thought of him being unkind and ugly. She may have said a few insulting things to the *real* king. "Oh no. What have I done?"

At last, Matthias released a hearty laugh, shoulders shaking, and the entire group of soldiers glanced their way. Including Quinn.

The *actual* king held her gaze across the field, and her stomach dipped as if she'd missed a step on her way down a staircase. She could imagine her face was bright red from embarrassment. But Quinn only gave her that beautiful half-smile of his and the faintest greeting with a lift of his fingers at his side.

"No harm done," the man said. "I assure you that it takes a lot to offend King Thistlethorn. Life beat his pride out of him at a young age. He does not take offense easily."

"I just…what is…I don't…" She clutched her hands to her heart as her gaze trailed Quinn's movements as he sparred with the soldiers, instructing them with the sword. "I understand very little, Matthias."

"I can imagine the last few days have been a whirlwind for you. Let me start the story at the beginning."

She cast him a dubious look. "Will this be short and sweet like Quinn's story? He is not the best storyteller."

Matthias laughed again as he shook his head. "He prefers bluntness and getting straight to the point to flowery words." He cleared his throat and stared out over the field as if being transported somewhere in the past. "Nineteen years ago, the Shades befell a great tragedy. The king was assassinated, stabbed while he was holding *your* seed, Briar. He accidentally dropped you over the ledge. Quinn, six at the time, dove over the ledge and caught you. He saved your life. But…he was not able to catch himself.”

Icy melancholy spread through her body as she finally connected the pieces of the puzzle. “His wings…”

He nodded. “One of his wings broke. Saving your life came at a steep price. To never fly again… It crushed him. He’d only ever dreamed of becoming the fastest flier in all of Eliandor.”

Guilt wormed its way into her heart. She knew it wasn’t her fault, but she couldn’t help but mourn what had happened to him. But she was also awed that he had done such a brave thing at such a young age.

The man continued. “Half of the assassins were subdued. The other half fled. But unfortunately, Quinn was just too young to protect you from so many threats. A bird ended up stealing your seed, and he has since sent guards to search for you every day for nineteen years. It was a miracle we found you.” His fingers clenched at his side and then relaxed once more. “Just in time, too.”

“It’s because of Laelynn,” she whispered, sending a silent prayer of gratitude to the helpful cat.

“Who?”

“A friend who told me to move my flower so I would be seen. I didn’t realize she was trying to help you find me.” Although moving her flower had almost killed her, it had given her the chance to find her people. “And what about this marriage?”

Once again, her attention fixed on Quinn as he shed his outer coat and tossed it to the side before resuming his spar with another soldier. His muscled arms flexed with each movement of the sword. With each block and parry.

And then her gaze landed on his wings. The upper wing on his right side was partially missing while the rest was worn and tattered.

All because he'd protected her seed.

Matthias's voice broke her out of her melancholy thoughts. "You two were bonded that tragic day. Once married, you were to be the other half of his magic, to help him protect our people. The Flares, which are our people," he gestured to her with his hand, "and the Shades. So, when you were dying days ago, he had to marry you straightaway to share his life's energy with you, to keep you from succumbing to the grave until your flower became more stable. His focus was on your flower. It was far too close to death. Hence the proxy marriage. He feels terrible about it. But there had been no other choice."

"I see…" She trailed a finger along the post, her eyebrows drawn together as she felt the smooth wood with her palm. It was too much to take in at once. The Flares? Magic? Marriage bond? "Are my parents still alive?"

"Yes. And your brother, Gabriel. They have been made aware that we found you. They are all but storming through our lands, demanding to see you. But we are making them wait until you are more stable." He winced and glanced in the opposite direction. "And it would help if you can demonstrate your magic, even the slightest bit. Otherwise, I fear they will continue to believe you are a fake."

"Relations between our people can't be so terrible that they'd accuse Quinn of lying."

"Oh, but they are. Your absence has been hard on all of us."

"I don't know any magic."

"Quinn will teach you. When you are ready." He paused. "Unless you think a more capable candidate will suit Shadowfalls better."

"I-I-I-I can't." She covered her face with her hands when another heated flare washed through her body and settled in her face.

"Can't…what?"

But she couldn't speak the words to answer out loud. *I can't possibly be the person they think I am. I can't do magic. I'm not a princess. I can't be married to a beautiful pixie king when I am no one. When I would sooner fail than succeed.*

When overwhelming emotions crashed into her at every side, she spun around and ran back down the path leading to the pond. Back toward the palace. Back toward the safety of her flower in the grove. As soon as her bare feet hit the lush soil of the quiet garden, she climbed up the fragile stem of the goldenblush and dove into the center of the flower.

Despite its weakness, the petals folded over her and hid her from view, keeping her safe from the outside world. She buried her face in the soft center and allowed herself to cry.

In the space of a few days, her entire world had turned upside down. And she wasn't sure what step to take next.

CHAPTER EIGHT

"SHE'S STILL IN THERE?" Quinn murmured quietly, arms crossed as he stood at the edge of his flower grove, the moonlight shining overhead during the peak of nocturnal activity for Shades. The goldenblush was still weak, but strong enough to house Briar. However, several petals were still missing, revealing the obvious gown sticking out at the side and small toes peeking out from beneath the hem.

If she was trying to hide, she wasn't doing a great job of it.

"I need you to speak to her." He grabbed his sister by the shoulders and pushed her toward the flower. But Cassie dug her heels into the ground, fighting against him and twisting out of his grip.

Her wings fluttered as she huffed, flipping her short black hair out of her eyes. She jabbed him in the chest with a finger and said in a hissing whisper, "Briar is *your* wife, Quinn! *You* need to form a connection with her.

Not me. As much as I wish to be her friend, *you* need to be that person for her right now. Otherwise, your marriage might never survive."

"I can't!" he shouted a little too loudly, as Briar's foot darted quickly into the confines of her flower, disappearing from sight. He rubbed a hand up and down the smooth leather sleeve of his coat, his gaze far away as he stared at the brilliant light of the moon overhead. "I can't, Cassie," he repeated. "Briar does not want to be married to me. She ran away," he gestured to her flower with both hands, "after she learned I was her husband and not Matthias."

He wanted to pull his curtain of hair over his eyes and disappear into a small wisp of smoke. Much preferable than facing the terrifying beauty before him.

He felt awful about not immediately revealing his identity to her when she'd first awoken. But he'd incorrectly assumed she'd caught on to who he was. Plus, he'd been flustered and insecure, and something about her had brought out the teasing levity within him. He'd made a mistake, and now he didn't know how to rectify his actions.

"How can I be what she wants?" His voice cracked, and he tried to disguise it with a cough. "Especially when she disapproves of me already?"

Cassie patted his elbow, lending him comfort with the simple touch. "Then don't be what she wants. Be what she *needs*. I know you want love in this marriage, Quinn.

But perhaps that's not what she needs right now. I think she desperately needs a friend."

He released a long, slow breath, his gaze lowering to the ground. Was he so obvious? And was it so wrong to want love? What if she never grew to love him? What if she didn't want to be married to him at all?

All his life, his concern had been for his people. And now? A little bit remained for himself. But if he wanted to reach Briar, he knew he needed to let it go. At least for a short time.

Taking a deep breath to steel his courage, he approached the goldenblush with hesitant footsteps. As a Flare pixie, she was likely sleeping, as they were diurnal whereas Shades were nocturnal. That was also an issue he wasn't entirely sure how to overcome.

He cleared his throat. "Briar?"

"Yes?" she answered after a moment's hesitation, her voice small and uncertain. Similar to how he felt, too.

"May I join you? I just want to talk."

At the end of the grove, Cassie gave him a thumbs up and a bright, cheery smile.

Another pause. This one longer.

When his hopes started to deflate, he turned away, only for her to finally answer with another, "Yes." He snapped his attention back to the flower, nearly injuring his neck.

Cassie faded into the shadows, leaving him by his lonesome with his unhappy wife. As much as he hated it… If he wanted Briar to open up to him, he, too, must make himself vulnerable in her presence.

A self-conscious shiver raked down his spine as he shed his outer coat, placing his wings on full display. It was his greatest insecurity. But if she were to know him, she must know all of him.

After taking another calming breath, he carefully climbed her weak bloom and slipped through an opening in the golden petals. The interior of the flower was soft and roomy, allowing him to sit across from Briar with plenty of room still between them. The bloom was cozy and bright, a stark contrast to his own. He reckoned he wouldn't want to leave, either, if the outside world was unfamiliar.

Across from him, Briar turned her head away as she rested her cheek on her knee, her arms wrapped around her legs. But his nocturnal vision didn't miss the red puffiness of her eyes as if she'd been crying for a while. A long while.

He bit his lip, staring down at his hands as he tried to figure out something to say. He had never been good at comforting others, and he felt rather inadequate in this situation.

"I apologize for waking you," he finally said, furiously scratching his head in frustration at himself for his insensitivity. "I'm nocturnal. I should have done this during the day. I can come back later."

"I was already awake," she said, stopping him from slipping back out of the flower. "What do you wish to talk about? Umm…Your Highness."

Her voice sounded flat but with the faintest hint of a tremor. She was afraid. Of him?

Matthias had said he'd told her everything. What more could he say?

"Can I answer any questions you have? And don't you dare skirt around my feelings. I can handle whatever you toss my way."

Briar lifted her head, the green of her eyes briefly meeting his before she glanced away again. "How do you know that seed was me? I could be anybody."

"Oh." He couldn't believe he'd glossed over this important detail. Well, actually, he could. He was terrible with details, after all.

He pulled up his sleeve and held out his forearm, slowly turning it around to show her the green vines from the bonding brand. "I've had this since the moment we were bonded. I saw yours when I found you unconscious in that human's house. They are supposed to reflect the color of each other's eyes." He chuckled nervously when she inspected her own brand before her gaze shot up to his eyes. "I'm immensely glad I wasn't born with a vomit-brown color."

The comment rewarded him with the faintest smile before she inspected his brand next. Though, she didn't touch him.

"There was no mistaking it was you." But then he grimaced. "May I speak frankly? I don't want to upset you in any way."

"I am tougher than you give me credit for."

He nodded once. "I suspected you were. How have you been able to survive for so long on your own? Away from our people?"

"I'm rather fast at running," she jested, but a part of him suspected it was true.

And another part…

Could her magic have protected her somehow? Her magic was supposed to lay dormant within her until they were married, only activated after he touched her bare skin. But could it somehow have helped her?

"Speaking frankly, sire?" she reminded him.

"Ah. Yes." He traced the leafy brand along his arm to avoid looking her way. "My father…" He cleared his throat. "He was assassinated when I was six. And therefore, I inherited his magic and his title at too young of an age. My magic allows me to place a protection barrier around our land, to protect our people. But it's weak without my other half. Well…" He chuckled nervously once more. "Actually, my magic is completely gone now. Our people are in danger. There are so many predators out there…"

When he glanced up, he found her frowning. "I expected an insult. Where is the frankness, Quinn?"

He more furiously rubbed the brand, not wanting to hurt her feelings but needing her to know, nonetheless. "A bonding is nearly permanent. Very little can break it. But I tried many times. So I could take another mate. To share the magic. Because no one could find you. And I care about my people immensely. But now you're here. And I'm terrified. For…for so many reasons."

She reached for him, but he quickly snatched his hand away, holding it away from her.

"I apologize," she rasped, folding her hands in her lap once more as her cheeks took on a rosier hue.

"Don't apologize. The moment you touch me, you will activate your half of the magic. I want you to have a choice."

"What choice is there?" she jested again, this time more feebly. Resigned. And terrified. Like himself.

Releasing a long breath, he placed his hands in his lap, palms up, to give her that choice once more. "There is *always* a choice, Briar. I want you by my side. I want you to get to know our people. To love them as I do. And I want you to know…that if you choose me, too, I will be by your side. Always." He paused once more to gather his emotions. "I had to learn my magic by myself. And it was terribly difficult. But you won't be forced to endure the same."

She stared at his hands as if contemplating a future with him, whatever that looked like. He still didn't know himself. If it must only be friendship, then so be it.

"What sort of princess wears rags all her life?" she asked. "Running for her life day after day? Knows nothing except survival and hardships? I want to belong here. It's all I've ever dreamed of—to find others like me. But…I'd be a fraud at your side. I fear I do not belong despite desperately wanting to."

"How could you possibly not belong?" He leaned forward with his elbows resting on his knees and offered a reassuring smile. "We've all been beside ourselves trying to locate you. Your parents are still heartbroken beyond belief. Everyone is *relieved* you are here. Our beloved golden princess."

"A-a-and you? You've wanted to break our bond for a while, it seems. I don't want to be the cause of your unhappiness."

He shook his head. "It never had anything to do with you. Rather a desperation to protect pixiekind. Being bonded to you doesn't make me unhappy, I assure you."

Rather the opposite, in fact. But he didn't dare tell her he liked her as more than a friend. She was beautiful and resilient, and she made his heart beat fast and his skin prickle with heat.

But like Cassie said, she didn't need a lover. She needed a friend.

"I know it's a lot to ask to help share my burden," he continued when she bit her lip, still not giving him an answer. "But I need you, Briar. I cannot do this without you." His shoulders slumped. He'd always tried to be strong. To prevent others from witnessing the chips and cracks in his soul. But tonight… "I'm so tired. Without the balance of our magic… Please."

What more could he say? He wanted this to be her choice. But if she didn't choose him, if she didn't choose her magic, then he feared for the safety of their people.

He felt helpless. So much burden had been placed on his shoulders with no one to help share it. He knew it was unfair to ask her to shoulder it with him. But what choice did he have?

An exhausted breath escaped his lips as he closed his eyes. The goldenblush briar was so cozy that he wanted to curl up on his side and fall asleep for the next week. Pixies slept in both beds indoors and in their flowers. He'd never considered sleeping in someone else's flower until today.

"Your happiness is important, too, Quinn," she finally said, and he cracked his eyes open to find her offering a shy smile. His stomach fluttered at the beautiful sight, and he quickly squashed it lest he manage to catch more feelings and break his own heart in the end. "I will accept the burden if it will help. Also…I do have one request."

"Anything," he breathed, too late realizing that promising anything might be next to impossible depending on her demand.

Another shy smile. "I spent days thinking I was married to Matthias. You never bothered to correct me."

He laughed and shook his head. "I feel terrible about that, and I'm sorry. I was just trying to tease you, but it did not exactly go the way I'd planned. It was a…difficult topic to broach. I know Matthias is wonderful and whatnot. But I hope I'm not too bad, either." Now he was teasing her again, though a bit of his insecurity must have leaked through his tone, as her expression softened into another smile.

"Our marriage doesn't quite feel real because of the proxy. My request is that we have a real ceremony. Me and you. One where I'm not halfway unconscious."

His chest filled with warmth. "I would like that as well."

And as he offered his hands once more, she didn't hesitate as she slipped her fingers into his. He tried to ignore the flutter of his stomach. The racing of his pulse. The warmth spreading up his arms.

Friend. Briar was a friend.

A burst of power exploded from him, following the link of their hands, and entered her with an intense surge of energy. She gasped and tried to jerk her hands away, but he held on tighter. To break the connection meant a weaker transfer of power.

An uncomfortable heat rushed through his blood as the connection between them restored his magic and gave Briar her own. Her fingers trembled in his. For a moment, her eyes glowed with a golden shimmer.

And then slowly, the surge of power faded, remaining within reach in each of them but waiting in a calm manner rather than with impatient excitement.

"N-n-now what?" Briar's teeth chattered as if the sudden loss of heat left a frigid chill in its wake.

"Now, I will teach you your magic. However, I don't wish to overwhelm you. The barrier of my magic around our land physically keeps threats out. Your magic will spread farther than mine, confusing the minds of those who venture near and encouraging them to turn a different way."

But for now, he could repair the barrier, and it was enough.

"But before we practice magic…" He reluctantly released her hands and leaned back, away from her. "Your family would like to meet you at sunrise. Are you feeling up to it?"

She nodded, rubbing a hand up and down her bonding brand while her gaze was far away. "Matthias said they will think I'm a fraud if I don't showcase my magic."

"They can think whatever they wish, but it does not change the truth that you are who I know you are, and that you do have an identical bonding mark to mine on your arm. Our relations between kingdoms are strained. Though, I hope we can begin to mend the rift now that you're here."

She bit her lip. "You are placing a lot of faith in me."

"Because I know you can do this." He didn't mention his inner worries to try not to overwhelm her. But he suspected her family would try to take her away from him. Given the choice, would she choose them? Or him?

Releasing a long breath filled with visible tension, she nodded. "Then at sunrise, I'll be ready."

The last thing he wanted was to leave her side, but he forced himself to climb back down her flower and keep his feet firmly planted on the ground. "Matthias and several other guards will always be nearby even when I can't." He pointed to the guards in question blending quietly in with the gates, far enough away to keep from overhearing their conversation but close enough to keep an eye on her. "I'll see you at sunrise."

"Wait!" she called after him as she climbed down from the flower and stopped before him. She clasped her hands in front of her and stared down at their feet. "Thank you."

Warmth filled his chest as he realized her gratitude encompassed more than just a friendly chat. "Thank *you*."

Before he could try to reach out and touch her, to pull her into an embrace, he turned and strode away, always and forever grounded to the floor, the skies forever out of reach without help. For so many years, he'd mourned the loss of his flight. But today…

He was relieved his loss hadn't been in vain.

CHAPTER NINE

BRIAR STARTLED AWAKE when something slammed in her room. She shot upright in her bed, eyes bleary as she glanced around the area until her gaze landed on a pixie with short black hair and shimmery purple wings.

Cassie.

Quinn's sister looked a lot like him but with short hair and feminine features. She wore black leather trousers and a black leather top that was strapped over one shoulder.

Did everyone here wear black?

As if attuned to her thoughts, Cassie tossed several outfits onto the foot of the bed before she continued to rummage through the armoire. "Many Shades prefer wearing darker colors. But considering the dress you came to us in… I assume you like lighter colors similar to most Flares."

Pulling back her bed sheets, she glanced down at the dress she still wore. She'd left her flower last night to sleep in the bed, but she felt disoriented all the same. "Is something wrong with what I'm wearing?"

The other woman gave her a sympathetic look as she tossed another dress onto the bed. "You've been wearing it for days, Briar, even in your unconscious state. It's time to change. Besides, you're meeting with your parents in a short hour. You and Quinn must put up a regal front."

Suddenly, Briar felt as if she treaded the unforgiving waters of a river, trying her best to keep her head above the surface when she was drowning. "I don't understand your culture yet."

Cassie turned and leveled her with a stare. "My brother is absolutely certain they will try to take you away today. Away from him. Away from us." She opened a drawer and rummaged through that next. "First it will be a friendly invite. And then they will make excuses for you to stay longer in Mapleborough. Soon enough, we'll rarely see you. They won't give you away so easily."

"Are they..." She bit her lip. "Unkind?"

Wicked was the word she wanted to say, but she dared not voice her fears.

Thankfully, Cassie shook her head. "We're not on the friendliest terms with them when our people used to be at war with one another. But we try to be amicable. They'll still try to take you, however."

The Shade pulled out something from the drawer and clacked them together. Briar's eyes shot wide open in shock when she found herself staring back at a beautiful pair of brown boots with laces climbing up the footwear like vines.

Briar leaped to her feet and flew across the room, taking the boots from her and spinning around in delight. "I can hardly believe they come in my size!"

"Have you never worn shoes before?"

"Never!"

After choosing a light green dress to match her eyes with a blue sash, Cassie instructed her on how to wear stockings and lace up her boots. Briar could hardly contain her excitement as she admired the ensemble in the full-length mirror, and then she rushed out of her room and down the stairs where Quinn waited in the main room.

"Quinn!" she giggled as she spun and lifted the hem of her skirts to reveal her footwear. "Can you believe it? I'm wearing shoes!"

She didn't miss the confused glance he cast toward his sister, and the faintest raise of his eyebrow.

Cassie squeezed her shoulders and explained, "She's never worn them before."

"Oh." His gray-purple lips lifted in an amused smile as he took her hand and spun her in another circle. "You certainly chose well. It's refreshing seeing something other than black."

Laughing, she poked him in the chest, still beaming with happiness over something so simple. "Yet, you wear it every day."

He lifted his black cloak to reveal the purple hue hiding beneath. "Purple." And then he pointed to his black, woven metal crown and the purple gems within it. "Purple. See, Briar? I don't always imitate midnight."

The sight of his half-smile stole her breath away, and for a moment, she floundered for words. Because he was both safe and terrifying. His presence filled her with comfort. But it also caused pricks of nervous energy to climb her body and settle in her face as heat. He almost perfectly embodied her parchment pixie, but he was even more handsome in real life than she could possibly express.

And then her world halted along with her breath as he produced a metal-woven crown similar to his but gold and studded with green gems. He gently slipped it over her head and placed it over her brow. It fit perfectly, as if made specifically for her.

"My queen," he murmured, dipping his head moments before he lifted her hand and kissed her fingers.

"I-I-I'm no queen."

"You were the princess of Mapleborough. But now you are the queen of Shadowfalls."

She shook her head, trying once again to keep her head above figurative waters. "There was no coronation."

"You became Queen the moment you received your half of the magic."

Cassie cut in. "And when you display your magic before our people in a more official ceremony, it will seal your position in Shadowfalls."

Briar pressed her lips together, running her fingers over the golden strands of her hair while focusing on taking deep breaths. Quinn had promised to stay by her side, that he wouldn't abandon her. And she trusted his word.

They exited the palace and followed the familiar path leading to the training grounds with Cassie and Tamara following farther behind to accompany them to the reunion. She gasped in fright at the sight of a crow and a swallow in the field and promptly ducked behind Quinn. But no one else seemed frightened of the birds, nor did they try to attack the creatures or flee.

"It's all right," Quinn reassured as he approached the crow and placed a hand on its feathered wing. A harness and saddle were attached to the bird in a similar fashion to a horse when ridden by a human. "He won't harm you."

"But they're birds."

He patted the creature again, and it cawed affectionately. "Birds can be loyal creatures if you treat them right. I've had this one since I was ten."

He offered his hand, and she approached slowly, eyeing the bird the entire time, worried it might strike out at her and swallow her whole.

When Quinn's warm grip and calloused fingers closed around hers, he guided her hand toward the bird, and together, they stroked the soft black feathers. A smile lifted her lips as she allowed him to continue to guide her hand down the feathers with each caress. The bird was soft and sleek, and it appeared to enjoy the attention.

But then she panicked as Quinn mounted the creature with one swoop of his leg and held his hand out again. She shook her head and stepped back, hands clasped over her heart. "I won't fly with you."

"How do you think you got here in the first place?"

"I was unconscious. It doesn't count."

"It's a long walk to the border."

"I'm sure I can manage."

He stopped arguing long enough to ask, "Why are you afraid?"

She glanced from the saddle strapped to the bird to the boughs high above and to the dark gray clouds overhead. One drop from the skies could injure her terribly or worse. "I don't want to fall."

"I will never let you fall." With his head, he gestured to the other soldiers and traveling companions around them. "And if by some miracle you do, someone would catch you. I promise, you are safe with us."

All her life, Briar had faced difficult things. She'd had to fend for herself, protect herself, live with the constant worry that each day might be her last. But now, she had a safety net. Perhaps even literally. And she trusted Quinn. He wouldn't let her fall.

Trudging through the muck of her fear, she grasped at the courage Quinn offered within his hand, and in a swift movement, he pulled her onto the back of the crow and held her tight around the waist in front of him.

Briar's heart squeezed in surprise at the strength of his arms around her, at his warmth seeping into her back, at how safe and secure she felt in his grip. The magical connection passed between them, tethering their souls to one another and creating a strong bond unlike any other. It was as if they were weaved from the same loom, forever connected in a series of thousands of threads to make a single picture, interwoven with strength and resilience.

She could trust him with her life. She knew it without a doubt.

The bird spread its wings and leaped into the air. Briar stifled a scream as she squeezed her eyes shut. Wind whipped through her hair. A fierce gust fluttered the hem of her gown around her legs. And only when the flight smoothed and the wind ceased its chaotic movement did she dare peek her eyes open.

A gasp escaped her lips when she found herself weaving between the boughs with the graceful tip of the bird's wings. In and out. Up and down. A dip of her stomach as the creature swooped through the air.

When the initial shock of the launch subsided, she laughed in delight, holding her arms out on either side of her when she felt safe and secure with Quinn's arms around her waist.

For a moment, she imagined she was flying with her own two wings secured to her back. The freedom of the skies beckoned her, holding her captive in a way she never knew could exist. It was exhilarating.

If only her human friend Priscilla could see her now. One day, she wanted to visit the girl again. Today was not that day.

She glanced over her shoulder, but her heart caught when she didn't realize exactly how near Quinn was. Her breath faltered at finding him close enough to see the subtle gray star patterns within his violet eyes. Close enough to feel his heart beating against her. Close enough to inhale his earthy, foresty scent.

A sharp turn snapped her attention back to the skies around them, and she was grateful for the distraction to hide the heat welling in her cheeks.

Slowly, the crow circled as it descended. Lower. Lower. Until it landed gracefully on the ground with a flap of its wings. Shade pixies landed around them, providing a barrier of protection as they dismounted from the crow.

For a moment, Briar was unsteady on her feet, unused to the foreignness of flying through the air. But as her balance righted, Quinn placed a hand on the small of her back and led her down a dirt path weaving through a colorful array of white, purple, and pink wildflowers on either side of them.

And when they rounded the bend...

She stopped short. At least two dozen soldiers waited behind three regally dressed Flare pixies with blonde and light brown hair, each wearing crowns of gold bands across their foreheads, similar to her own.

Briar's stomach twisted with anxiety the moment she recognized herself in the woman with blonde hair. It was as if she looked into a mirror but one that aged her twenty years. Her father must have been the one with the red-brown beard, and she assumed the dark blonde pixie standing tall with a look of discontent on his face was her brother, Gabriel.

The king, Florian, her father, ran a hand over his beard and began tearing up. The queen, Ophelia, rested a hand over her heart, her green eyes wide with either distress or shock, she wasn't sure.

"Briar!" her mother gasped, taking a single step forward but stopping herself. If she crossed the border between their lands without permission, Quinn had mentioned it was bad diplomacy and could cause more harm than good. "Let me see you."

She took several steps closer and turned in a full circle, feeling self-conscious that dozens of eyes were fixed on her. Meeting her parents should have elated her. But they were near strangers. She knew hardly a thing about them. And she wasn't quite sure how to react in their presence.

"Has she displayed her magic?" her father asked Quinn as he glanced over her shoulder.

With a shake of his head, Quinn answered, "Not yet. But it's there."

"We've spent years searching for her. How did you…"

"Perhaps fairy godmotherly intervention. We were lucky."

Oftentimes, the fairies in Eliandor were up to nothing but mischief to serve their own needs. But Laelynn had seemed different. She'd helped rather than hindered.

Ophelia held out her arms, and even though Briar had never met this woman, she felt an emotional tug toward her. As if her spirit had known her long before now.

But when she stepped forward, Quinn caught onto her wrist. Under his breath, he murmured in her ear, "If you step over that line, I cannot physically bring you back. I cannot help you if you need help."

"Am I in danger?"

"I don't know, Briar. Someone is out for our blood. I don't know who to trust."

Although he seemed to doubt the king and queen were capable of hurting their own daughter… Those red-cloaked guards had gotten into the palace somehow all those years ago. It could have been a guard or an advisor or a servant who had betrayed them, who had instructed them how to sneak into the palace. From what she'd learned, her parents had tried for a long time to conceive another child. It made no sense for them to do away with their own daughter.

"But I am safe with you." It wasn't a question but rather a statement.

"Always."

Even though she knew he would defend her, even to the point of losing the one thing he cared about most in this world—his flight—she knew she could not cower behind him. Especially if she were to be the queen of the Shades.

All her life, she had grown up alone but had relied too heavily on the help from Laelynn, Priscilla, and even Quinn. She wanted to find her own strength and make her own decisions. To start being the queen her people needed her to be.

Therefore, she pushed past her uncertainty, stepped over the boundary line, and crossed the distance between them. She threw her arms around her mother's neck first, holding on tight to the warm comfort she offered with her presence alone. The embrace was familiar. As if her seed remembered her gentle touch long before she'd sprouted.

Next, she embraced her father, and when the man burst into loud sobs, she couldn't help but tear up at their reunion as well. She didn't have to know her parents to love them.

And then she turned to her older brother, taking in his rigid posture and his crossed arms. The cold distrust in his eyes. Perhaps over time they might be able to form a friendship. But he certainly didn't seem open to the idea currently.

A crash of thunder overhead startled them apart, and Briar glanced toward the skies with panic rushing through every breath. The scent of a storm lingered in the air, and the clouds seemed to have grown darker in the past few minutes.

The rain! They must seek shelter from the rain.

But unlike her, the others didn't seem too worried about the promise of a downpour. However, they were at least concerned enough to retreat indoors immediately.

"Come," her mother said with a squeeze to her hand. "Visit the palace with us. I want to show you what your life would have been like had you grown up here. I want you to see your home."

Cassie's words from earlier echoed in her mind. A warning.

"First it will be a friendly invite. And then they will make excuses for you to stay longer in Mapleborough. Soon enough, we'll rarely see you. They won't give you away so easily."

The question remained… Did she want to embrace the safety and love of her parents? Or did she want to find out what a life at Quinn's side would bring? Already, she loved the people of Shadowfalls. At least the ones she had met. And Quinn…

She hardly dared to hope for future happiness in their marriage. And perhaps…even love.

As she glanced over her shoulder to find Quinn's steely expression fixed on her, she realized he was giving her a choice. Because that's all he'd ever tried to do—offer a choice even when the future was sealed. Even when the only path was forward.

Another rumble of thunder.

She returned her attention to her parents, realizing she needed to make a quick decision. Quinn or her parents? Was it possible to have both? Or must she choose now?

Finally, Briar offered a warm smile. "Quinn and I would love nothing more than to see the palace."

Her parents glanced at each other, their discontent showing on their faces just as Cassie had suggested. Did they not like Quinn because he was her husband? Or because he was a Shade?

But glancing out of the corner of her eye, she found Quinn's mouth twitching as if trying to restrain his amusement. Thankfully, he did not appear offended.

"We would love to have the two of you," her mother answered in a strained tone. She nodded to Quinn. "You have our permission to cross the—"

Lightning lit up the skies in a brilliant light, quickly followed by a crash of thunder directly over their heads. For a moment, the searing light stunned her, and when she blinked back the disorienting flash in her eyes…

That's when she noticed the red cloaks.

CHAPTER TEN

FOR YEARS, QUINN had trained intensively with magic and a wide array of weapons, waiting for the day he might have to defend his people from the Red Cloaks. Nineteen years ago, he hadn't been ready.

But today, he was prepared.

In a flash of movement, he drew his sword and blocked his first opponent's strike in a clash of steel on steel. Red fabric billowed in a fierce breeze. The hood of the cloak lifted just enough for him to catch a glimpse of a long chin. But then his attention shifted to his footwork as he struck with his weapon. Not to practice. Not to spar. But to protect.

After he felled his first opponent, he frantically searched for Briar and found her on the opposite side of the border, too far out of reach. If he crossed the border in any way without explicit permission, he could bring war between their kingdoms.

Another Red Cloak charged toward him with his sword drawn. Quinn lifted a hand and reached for the magic straining against its leash within him. His power eagerly charged down his arm, into his hand, and he shot a blast of purple magic at the man. It hit him squarely in the chest, sending him flying backward until he crashed into the tree and slumped to the ground in a heap of red fabric.

"Matthias!" he shouted, searching for his second in command. He expected to find the man in the center of the fight but instead located him beside the birds, holding them by the reins and trying to keep them from flying away. Matthias glanced up at the sound of his name, and when Quinn ordered him to protect Briar, as he was a Flare and could cross the border without consequence, he abandoned the birds altogether and rushed with his sword in his hand across the border and in front of Briar.

Quinn's heart shot to his throat when Matthias lifted his weapon above Briar's head. In the split of a moment, he didn't care if he brought war between their people. Nothing else mattered but Briar. After searching for her for years, he realized he did not want to—*could not*—live without her. If the consequence was death or war, then so be it.

His power raced down his arm. But before he released it, Matthias turned his weapon at the last moment and sparred with a figure in a red cloak. For a moment, he'd thought the man he trusted more than anything had planned to kill his wife. The angle must have been deceptive.

Rather than slamming his magic into Matthias, Quinn redirected it toward another enemy on his side of the border, felling his opponent with a single blast of purple.

His grip tightened on his sword as he fought against the other Red Cloaks on his side of the border, ducking lethal swings and parrying deadly stabs. The battlefield was a dance of feet, cloaks, and weapons, the rolling thunder and clashing blades the music to the performance.

Big, fat raindrops fell from the sky, some of them half his size. They splashed to the ground around him, water quickly soaking through his clothing and clinging to his hair. Instead of one opponent, he now faced two as he tried to dodge the downpour from above.

Lightning flashed across the skies once more, momentarily blinding him. Pain seared his arm as a weapon sliced through his skin. In his brief moment of disorientation, something slammed into his chest, and he stumbled backward closer to the drop-off leading down to the river rushing below.

Too slow, he lifted his sword to block the next attack. He braced himself for the bitter sting of death. But rather than feeling the tip of a sword slam through his chest, a branch swung from the side and smashed against the back of the enemy's head.

The man collapsed to the ground, revealing Briar standing behind with a branch in her hand and a look of desperation in her eyes.

At the same moment, they reached for each other. But only the tips of their fingers brushed when the soggy ground crumbled beneath him.

He yelped, the rain-soaked earth grabbing his legs and pulling him down a steep mudslide. He dropped his sword and clawed desperately at the raging mud. But the more he clawed, the more he buried himself. The earth climbed over his legs, his waist, and he barely managed to keep his arms and head above the soaking soil.

Panic ripped through his chest, heaving with each frantic breath as he stared at the lethal waters of the river growing closer by the second. No flutter of wings followed him, as his men were locked in battle and either hadn't seen him fall or couldn't reach him in time.

Water crashed against rocks below, deafening in his ears next to the rain and thunder surrounding him. He lent every ounce of his strength to escaping the mudslide, desperation in each movement as he tried to free himself.

But then the mud dragged him into the river with a chilly shock shooting through his body.

And in that moment, he realized he was going to die. Because he couldn't swim.

"Quinn!" Briar screamed the moment he disappeared beneath the water of the river.

She wasted no time as she sprinted down the steep slope, following a grassy path rather than the muddy portion when it was more stable than the other.

The moment her feet touched the bottom of the hill, she sprinted along the river, over small stones, and dodged between larger rocks. Grass and reeds lined the bank, acting as obstacles as she searched frantically for Quinn.

When she didn't find him, she ran faster until her legs protested and her feet ached within foreign shoes.

And as she rounded the bend in the river...

She caught sight of a head of black hair bobbing momentarily to the surface before dipping below the angry waters once more.

Briar took a running leap off a rock, the wind rushing through her hair before she splashed into the water right behind him.

The shock of the cold rushed through her body, but she pushed through as her fingers brushed against sodden fabric. She grabbed hold of Quinn's cloak and pulled herself closer until she managed to wrap her arms around his waist.

With a twist of her body, she propelled him closer to the surface until his head broke out of the water. He gasped in a breath, choking and sputtering when the small waves crashed over their heads, and the splash of rainwater hit them in the face.

"Briar!" he gasped, but then he started choking on the water again. It was almost as if he…

Couldn't swim.

She gritted her teeth as she realized she must be the one to get them out of the water. If she failed, they could both drown.

Fear pulsed through her when the water turned white and propelled them forward more rapidly. The heavy weight of the river slammed them into boulders and tangled them in reeds. Although he couldn't swim, Quinn lifted his hand enough to break the reeds with a surge of his magic before the water crashed over them once again.

A large wave smashed into them and pulled them under. They flipped beneath the surface, and more than once, Briar almost lost her grip on Quinn. But then by some miracle, they found the surface once more.

Briar frantically kicked with her legs to keep them from slipping under. Without the use of her arms, she found it difficult to do anything more than keep them afloat.

Quinn's damp hair pressed against her chin as she twisted more to make sure his head remained above the surface. His head flopped on her shoulder. Conscious but not quite as alert as before.

Her stomach tightened with dread when she spotted the stream of blood running from a gash in his hairline.

The way ahead nearly blinded her with white water and more rocks. But somehow, she found the energy she needed to cut a path through the shallow bend until her feet slipped on rocks rather than water. The river pushed her one way and then the other, threatening to pull her feet out from beneath her.

She gritted her teeth and fought against the current, focusing on taking one step in front of the other while dragging Quinn through the tempest. When his feet touched the ground, he was lucid enough to help her in the fight against the river. Together, they grabbed onto a nearby reed stretching over the bank, and little by little, they pulled themselves toward the shore until they slumped onto wet rocks in a heap of heavy, sodden fabric and gasping breaths.

But their relief was short lived when a raindrop hit her back and smashed her face into the ground.

She scrambled to her feet, grabbed Quinn by the arm, and together they sprinted in a dizzy zig zag when he could hardly remain upright. A hollow within an upright tree drew her attention. If they could only reach it, they could seek shelter until the storm ended.

The next raindrop smashed into Quinn's shoulder, collapsing him to his hands and knees. Another came at him at an angle and flipped him violently onto his side.

Briar screeched in fright when the torrent worsened with a bright flash and a clap of thunder. She flinched against the next strike from nature, throwing her hands over her head and squeezing her eyes shut.

But instead of getting pelted by enormous raindrops, the rain beat against a solid barrier overhead.

A gasp escaped her when she found a golden dome stretching over her head, protecting them from the storm. Raindrops hit the barrier with muted *thunks* before rolling down the side and splashing onto the ground.

"Don't drop your magic." Quinn grunted as he pushed himself to his feet and held her around the waist with one arm. Rather than continue their flight at a fast pace, they walked slowly to help her keep the barrier up with whatever concentration remained.

Finally, the gold dome flickered out right as they reached the safety of the tree. They slipped inside the crevice, and the first thing Quinn did was collapse to his knees.

"Quinn!" she cried, crouching beside him and placing her hands on either side of his face to inspect his injuries. A gash continued to bleed at his hairline. The shadow of a bruise appeared at the edge of his jaw. His eyes squeezed shut as if he found it difficult to focus on her.

"I'm all right," he insisted. "I just took a tumble."

That's when she noticed the blood soaking through the fabric of his sleeve in the dim light of the hollow. It wasn't a wound he'd sustained from the river. It was from the edge of a blade.

She tapped his hand. "I need a light."

He released a shuddering breath moments before purple magic flowed from the tips of his fingers and created balls of shimmering light floating aimlessly above their heads. The light illuminated the dried pine needles, leaves, and small stones tucked into the corners of the hollow, and it even revealed the gash in his arm.

Without waiting for permission, she snatched the knife she spotted tucked into his boot and carefully cut away the fabric of the sleeve on his injured arm. Next, she ripped several swaths of fabric from her underskirts and tried to clean the injury as much as possible before wrapping a long piece around his arm and tying it tight to staunch the bleeding. The fabric was wet, and she worried it would help very little because of it. But it was all they had.

"You've done this sort of thing before," Quinn said with a wince of pain around his eyes.

"Like I said, I've been on my own for a while. I had to learn to survive."

She handed another swath to him and instructed him to hold it against his head as she collected stones, pine needles, and dried leaves from the hollow around her. The bundle was nearly unwieldy in her arms, as large as the items were, but somehow, she managed.

She created a circle with the stones and broke off pieces of leaves and pine needles, strategically placing them inside. Over the kindling, she stacked dry twigs into a pyramid shape and sat back on her heels.

"Can you make a fire with your magic?" she asked.

He shook his head. "I've never been able to accomplish anything hot." His shoulders slumped, and he braced a hand against the ground as if hardly able to remain upright. "You are a Flare. If anyone can do it, it would be you."

"How?"

Rather than speaking when it seemed to pain him, he held out a hand with his palm faced downward to demonstrate. She mimicked him by holding both of her hands in the same position and trying to reach for her magic. Somehow, she'd been able to erect the barrier to protect them from the rain. Surely, she could perform a feat of magic again.

Her fingers began shaking, whether from the chill running rampant through her body from her soaked clothing or the shock of the event wearing off, she wasn't sure.

Therefore, she closed her eyes and concentrated. She *had* to do this. True, she could make a fire using a stick, but it could take a long time. Too long. Quinn needed warmth *now*.

Taking a deep, steadying breath, she allowed instinct to overpower her fear as she searched for her magic within her. She felt it as an overwhelming well filled with untapped potential. Right within reach. Waiting for her to take control.

But how?

Create fire, she demanded her magic.

Nothing.

She flicked her fingers as if flames might shoot from her fingertips. Still nothing.

Quinn needs my help. I must do this!

In an act of desperation, she reached for her magic but must have scooped up far too much. Fire shot from her hands and caught onto the kindling, but the excess burst into sparks around them. She cried out in alarm and lifted her hands to protect her face. And when the initial flash of heat dispersed, she opened her eyes to find embers scattered across the ground outside of the safety of the fire pit.

Launching to her feet, she stamped out each of the errant embers, grateful neither of them had caught fire when their hair and clothing were too soaked.

Quinn burst into laughter, which turned into groans of pain and more laughter as he held his side with one hand and his head with the other.

"Are you laughing at me?" She crossed her arms and glared at him as she stamped out the last flaming ember.

"No," he grunted, followed by a wheezing breath. "I'm laughing with you?"

Briar snorted and clamped a hand over her mouth, shaking her head as she tried to glare again but found herself unsuccessful when relief overpowered her anger and embarrassment. They had survived both the river and the attack from the Red Cloaks. Although they were good and stuck in the hollow until the rain abated, there certainly was worse company to keep.

Unable to hold still when work needed to be done, she located enormous dry leaves and placed them around the fire to use as a barrier between them and the ground. Quinn was able to maneuver himself onto one of the leaves while she strategically stacked larger branches to use to hang wet clothing to dry.

Carefully, she helped him out of his cloak, but then she gasped at the sight of his wings.

"Oh!" she cried, startled to find his broken, purple translucent wing edged with gold at the bottom as if the thin membrane had grown in the space of the last hour. The gold shimmered with each of his movements, appearing out of place on his back but a beautiful addition to the darker hue of his wings.

"What is it?" He turned his head to look at her, but she averted her gaze and placed her focus on draping his cloak over the branches. Droplets of water dripped from the soaked fabric and onto the ground.

"It's nothing," she lied. "I thought I saw another ember." She didn't know how his wing had healed the slightest bit, but she didn't want to get his hopes up if it would lead nowhere.

He grunted as he rolled onto his side, wincing with the movement. "You shouldn't have jumped in the river after me. You could have died."

"Yes, I could have. But so could you." But then she sobered as he pulled the red-soaked fabric away from his head. The injury had stopped bleeding, which indicated it must not have been as bad as it looked. "I'm so sorry I couldn't do more."

"Do more?" he scoffed. "You saved my life, Briar. And how could you blame yourself when it was us against the river?"

"But…" She knelt beside him and cut another piece of her underskirts, gently dabbing at his hairline wound. "I'm usually a better swimmer."

Again, he winced. "And I can't swim at all."

Her hand paused above the injury as she searched his eyes for a jest but found none. Sure, she'd suspected it, but to hear it confirmed? "Not at all?"

He shook his head. "Shades can't swim. Our wings don't like to be submerged. We are especially not adapted for rough waters." He chuckled but then groaned as he clutched his side. Through gritted teeth, he continued, "Flares can swim, and Shades can fly. We are well balanced between our kinds."

When concern rippled through her, she gently peeled his fingers away from his side and ignored his protests of optimal health as she lifted his shirt on the left.

She gasped when she found a large purple bruise over his ribs, the skin scraped and bruised and appearing all too painful to endure.

"What can my magic do?" Her hands fluttered uselessly over his wound, wanting to take away his pain but not daring to touch it. "Can it heal you?"

Never mind that she had no idea how to use her magic in the first place.

"I don't know." He breathed deeply through his nose, his fists clenching at his side.

"I thought you knew how my magic worked."

"All I have are accounts from those who saw it in action from my mother. I can only surmise what the rest might be, as the Red Cloaks burned our records many years ago."

"But…but…" She stared down at her hands, not knowing how she'd created the protective barrier and the fire nor how to accomplish the feat again. "Wouldn't you have learned about it from her?"

"My mother is dead." His voice quavered, whether from emotion or pain, she wasn't sure. "She died a couple years before my father did. Goblins killed her."

Briar sat back on her heels, studying the pained, grieving creases around his eyes. To lose both parents within a couple years…

"Quinn…" she murmured, not knowing what else to say, not knowing how else to give him comfort.

"I'm sure he thought he had more time as he searched for another wife to hold the other half of the magic. I was only six. How could I have known to prepare for his death?"

A sharp breath escaped her when he took her hand and placed it over his chest. His heart beat strong against her palm, reassuring her he was alive and on the mend. "My father never told me. I was too young to understand. But I ended up discovering it for myself."

"Discovering what?"

His grip on her hand tightened. He didn't look her way as he answered. "The war between our people started because of my father. When my mother died, his magic took on a mind of its own in his grief, in his anger. It...exploded. A tragic accident. But...many people died, both Flares and Shades. So many good people, including Matthias's family. That's why you and I were betrothed when we were little. The first royal match between our people. To stop the bloodshed. But it hasn't stopped."

Numbing shock coursed through her. If she hadn't jumped into the river after him, the war might have continued in earnest.

"Why didn't you tell me?"

"Because I'm scared, Briar!" His chin quivered as he finally pulled his gaze from the fire and looked her in the eye. "I'm scared. I've been alone for so long... I don't want to lose you."

Her fingers curled around his wet tunic at the confession, and she knew without a doubt that she didn't want to lose him, either. "Well..." She tucked a strand of hair behind her ear. "I suppose you are better than a paper cutout."

He laughed softly as if trying to avoid jostling his ribs. "That means a lot coming from you. I know how fond you are of it."

"Hardly," she scoffed playfully.

He dropped her hand to poke her in the ribs. "You were snuggling it when I found you at the human house."

Her cheeks flamed. "I was not."

"You were! It wasn't easy to transport it back home, as large as it was. But I wanted you to be happy. You know, in case you actually survived."

"And I did. Thanks to you."

"Then I suppose we're even." He squeezed her hand, and for a moment, she found herself unable to tear her gaze away from his black, sharp fingernails and the purple-gray hue of his skin.

So foreign and beautiful, unlike anything she had ever seen. She didn't even try to resist the urge to touch him, to brush her finger along his wrist to his thumb. Lightly, her fingertips traced the smooth purple of his skin, the grooves of each knuckle, and then she outlined the obsidian gleam of his pointed fingernails.

He lifted the same hand to capture her chin, the point of his fingernails cradling her tenderly. The breath caught in her lungs.

"Briar," he whispered.

Her name on his tongue felt like a soft caress, like a velvety promise not spoken out loud but through their hearts alone. He brushed his thumb along her bottom lip.

She held perfectly still. He leaned closer. Slowly. Almost as if asking permission.

But she could not give it. Because trusting someone fully, especially with her heart, terrified her.

She quickly pulled out of his grip and stood on shaky legs. "I-I-I need to check on the storm."

To hide her fluster, she turned her back to him and stood at the entrance of the hollow, staring outside at the pouring rain obscuring the nearby surroundings.

A warmth burned bright in her soul. Unfamiliar feelings stirred within her chest whenever she touched Quinn, whenever she found herself near him. They exhilarated her. They terrified her.

And she didn't know what to do with them.

She'd already lost so much. If she gave Quinn even the smallest sliver of her heart... Would he break it? Or was taking the running leap worth it should he keep her heart safe instead of shattering it?

A shiver raked over her body, and she hugged her arms to herself as she struggled to maintain her heat.

Quinn was no paper cutout. He was real. Significant. Consequential. And she feared giving him the power to both love her and break her. If she gave him her heart...

Would it shatter?

Or would it burn?

CHAPTER ELEVEN

WAITING OUT THE storm proved futile.

A night passed and rain continued to pour from the skies, the sheet so thick that it was impossible to see anything past the river aside from the silhouette of several trees and boulders. The river reeds protested the weight of each raindrop. The tree they took shelter in groaned against the wind.

Quinn frowned, his eyebrows creased with worry as he stared at the storm pounding ceaselessly outside their shelter from where he sat on his leaf bed, his elbow propped on his knee.

"Care to share what's on your mind?" Briar asked, pulling his gaze away from the exit and to where she stirred mushroom soup within the shell of an acorn hanging over the flames with a makeshift wooden spoon. Thus far, she'd only managed to surprise him with her resourcefulness. It was clear she'd had to learn to survive on her own.

And he hated it.

Well, he loved her survival skills. Hated that she'd had to learn them in the first place.

"My sister," he rasped, not sure how to continue his thoughts. If he entertained the idea… No. He mustn't believe she might be dead. "Cassie and I are close, especially since we only have each other aside from a few extended family members. I'm just worried… What if she didn't escape the fight?"

A sigh heaved from his lungs. He might have been able to prevent this. He'd known the Red Cloaks would make another attempt on his life. Or Briar's. He should have been more prepared. This was his fault.

"Cassie is stronger than you think." Briar scooped a portion of the soup into an empty acorn shell and handed it to him. Their fingers brushed, and he couldn't stop the tumult of emotions heating within his chest.

Embarrassment. Longing. Disappointment. Regret.

For some reason, he couldn't keep his head clear enough to remember Cassie's words, that Briar needed a friend. And *just* a friend. He shouldn't have tried to kiss her. He'd only set himself up for disappointment when she'd rejected his advances.

The bowl exchange ended all too quickly for his liking, and he placed his focus into taking a hesitant sip of the hot liquid.

"Oh!" He took another sip and savored the rich flavor of the mushrooms and the pleasant warmth of the broth. "This is actually good."

Briar chided him with a hand on her hip and a wave of her spoon in the air. "I'm not sure whether to be offended or flattered."

"Flattered. Most definitely."

He quickly finished off the soup, and his aching injuries felt marginally better afterward. Even his maimed wing didn't feel quite so lopsided.

He caught Briar's attention fixed on his wing, but she quickly glanced away and placed her focus on her own soup.

"We have nowhere to go until the rain stops." Her attention lifted from her bowl, and for the first time since his attempted kiss, she braved looking him in the eye. "Can you teach me how to use my magic?"

He shrugged one shoulder teasingly but instantly regretted the action when his side ached with protest. "It seems you are doing just fine intuitively reaching for your power."

"Quinn." She gave him an exasperated look. "I nearly blew us up trying to create a fire."

The wound in his side gave him sharp pains as he chuckled. "I'm not quite as fragile as you think I am." With an arc of his arm, he created a purple, shimmering barrier between them. The purple hue flickered out after a few moments.

"And you didn't use it in the river?"

"I'll admit my first instinct wasn't to use my magic."

"Then what was your first instinct?"

He pressed his lips together, keeping his mouth shut. How could he possibly explain the instinctual reaction for his wings to save him even when they no longer worked correctly?

A grunt escaped him as he pushed himself into a standing position and crossed the hollow to a larger area he intended for combat. Rain continued to beat against the tree, drowning out all noise from the outside world and confining them to the hollow, just the two of them.

Quinn was aware of every breath Briar took, every movement she made, and he knew it was a terrible idea to be stranded with her. But at least he could try to distract his thoughts from wandering past the line of friendship.

"Do it again," he said with a nod of his head. "Throw whatever magic you have at me."

"Quinn," she said again, this time in a strained tone. "I won't put your life in danger if I can help it."

"Briar." The calm use of her name washed some of the uncertainty from her features but not all of it. "The first step is finding your magic and using it without abandon. The second step is control. Do you trust me?"

Slowly, she stepped away from the billowing fire and joined him in his makeshift sparring arena. She took a deep, quavering breath and nodded. "I trust you."

Those three words were simple, but he cherished them, nonetheless. He wanted to prove himself worthy of her trust. To prove she could lean on him and place her faith in him. Despite his injuries, he refused to betray her trust in any way.

Before the use of any magic, he instructed her on stance, hand movement, and how to reach for her magic and keep it steady. It reminded him of the hours upon frustrating hours he'd spent on the field himself trying to hone his magic and figure out what he could do. Of course, the records of the strong, ancient magic had existed, but the Red Cloaks had burned them long ago. It was up to Briar and himself to rediscover what they could accomplish with the power.

A blast of golden magic shot out of Briar's hands, and she cried out in alarm. He quickly braced himself against his own protective barrier, obliterating her magic in a spark of gold and purple lighting up the hollow.

"Good," he praised, trying not to show amusement at the shock staring back from her wide eyes. "Try again. But hit me harder this time."

After several minutes of trying to harness her magic, frustration took hold of her features as she attempted the feat again and again without success. But then her magic slammed into his barrier harder than before, the force of it nearly knocking him off his feet.

He gritted his teeth, holding his magic steady and only allowing it to flicker out when the gold dispersed.

However, surprise crashed over him when another wave of gold shot toward him. He barely erected the barrier in time to block it before side-stepping the next attack. Burst after burst of gold shot toward him, and soon it became a dance of pixie against pixie, her on the offense and him on the defense.

Briar moved more swiftly as her confidence visibly grew before his eyes, and he couldn't help but whoop with excitement at her natural-born talent. She smiled wide as her movements and attacks became more precise, more controlled.

Perhaps it was the excitement, or maybe he thought she was ready to try, but he blasted his own magic toward her, and with a wide arc of her arm…

She blocked it with a shimmering golden shield.

Both stood in momentary stunned silence as her shield slowly flickered out, leaving them gasping for each breath in tune with the rain pounding outside the hollow.

"Briar." Her name escaped him as a breathy whisper as he tried to wrap his mind around how quickly she'd caught on. "You—"

The pungent scent of rot and warg feces stopped his words in his tracks. Panic clawed at his throat, taking him back to the dark day his mother had been killed. Flashes of green skin and warped tusks pounded in his skull. The stench. The rot. The desperate cries for help.

Quinn forced himself out of his stupor long enough to sprint the distance between himself and Briar. He grabbed her by the waist and pulled her against the inside wall nearest the door just as a large green hand as big as a bird tried to snatch her, missing by a hair's breadth.

"I almost got 'er!" a goblin outside the hollow exclaimed. His hand continued to fish around as it searched for them.

He held Briar tighter with her back pressed against his chest, trying to tuck them into the nearest crevice in the wood as much as possible. He felt her heart pounding against him, her pulse erratic and every quick breath filled with terror akin to his. By themselves, they were too small to take on such a large threat without other pixies to back them up in a fight.

The goblin hissed when its hand encountered the fire, the weight of it putting out the flames until only smoke remained. "Where are you lil' pretty?"

In his fear, Quinn found it difficult to use his magic. By some miracle, he reached for it within him and slowly erected a purple barrier around them, solidifying it with layers upon layers of magic. He wasn't sure if it would hold.

"Aw, get outta there!" another goblin growled, followed by what sounded like a kick. The first goblin grunted out a garble but continued to reach around the hollow until its hand came dangerously close to them.

"I'm tellin' you!" the goblin said. "I saw the pixies doin' their magic."

"There was nothin' there! Now let's tell them bosses we found them drowned in the river so they give us our reward." The creature cleared his throat in a sickening manner and spat somewhere outside. "Demanding pixies. I hates them all."

Quinn inhaled sharply at the revelation. At the abundance of recent goblin sightings right as the barrier was weakening. Right as Briar had returned home.

The goblins were working for pixies.

The goblin's fingers brushed against the erected barrier, and Quinn held his breath, backing up as much as possible while keeping a firm hold on Briar, trying not to make a single sound to give away their position.

Finally, the hand retreated from the hollow, and the goblins' heavy footsteps crunched against rocks and foliage, becoming fainter by the second until they disappeared altogether.

He released a long breath and slumped heavily against the wall. Fear continued to hold his arms captive, preventing him from dropping his grip on Briar. But he couldn't let go when his limbs were locked in place.

If he ever lost her...

His vision clouded over at the thought. He knew he wasn't supposed to. He *knew* it was a bad idea. But even after everything, he couldn't stop himself from falling for Briar in the end. From the very first moment he'd seen her, held her unconscious form in his arms, he'd known he would do anything to protect her. He admired her bravery, her unfailing spirit, her lack of judgment over the state of his wings. He should have seen how easily he would fall for her, to care for her unlike anything or anyone he'd ever cared for in his life.

Within the enclosure of his arms, Briar turned to face him. Her lips parted when her gaze landed on his face, and he squeezed his eyes shut to try to hide his tears but to no avail.

"I'm not enough," he said with a quaver in his voice.

"You *are* enough." She wiped the tears from his cheeks with her thumbs. "They didn't find us. We're safe."

"The Red Cloaks are in league with the goblins. I can't do this. I can't do it."

"No, you can't," she replied with a shake of her head before she stood on her toes and kissed his cheek, leaving a burning warmth where her lips had touched his skin. "But *we* can. We'll do this together."

Quinn blinked rapidly, overwhelmed by the support she offered him, by the comfort she gave with her words, with her presence.

He tightened his arms around her shoulders and pressed her against his chest, needing to hold her, needing to know she was whole and safe. She fit perfectly in his arms, almost as if she were meant to be there from the very beginning. As if she had always been meant for him and no one else.

His heart burned beneath her touch as she placed a hand over his chest and leaned back enough to look him in the eye. "Let's return home and give our people the hope they need."

CHAPTER TWELVE

BY THE TIME THEY dared to brave the elements with nothing but each other and their magic, the rain had stopped pouring from the skies and slowed down to a misty drizzle. Briar exited the tree's hollow hand in hand with Quinn, each holding tight to the other for comfort and strength.

Something had changed between them in the hideout. A subtle shift in feelings. A turn of their relationship. Yes, they were already married, but it didn't feel quite like a simple title anymore. They were companions. Two sides of the same coin. A unification of magic and purpose.

Briar peeked at Quinn out of the corner of her eye as he led her through a series of turns in a quiet, dewdrop forest. She admired his broad stance, his silent confidence, his sure steps. She adored the spark in his violet eyes, the smooth curve of his defined chin, the shape of his purple-black lips. Although he oozed confidence, she knew he was scared. But he pressed forward, anyway. Because despite how terrified he was for himself, he seemed to be more terrified for others.

They paused briefly in front of a pine tree acting as a fork in the road between two paths. Quinn adjusted his grip on her hand until he weaved his fingers more intimately with hers and led her down the path to the left.

Her heart tripped and stumbled within her chest. Her stomach tied itself in knots. A daze of excitement and nervousness clouded around her head at every place their hands touched, the gentle strength of his grip, the *caring* he showed her without saying a single word.

But then her good mood instantly vanished when she heard goblins' voices around the bend. And this time, there were more than two.

"Quinn," she warned, and he nodded with confirmation that he heard them, too. They weren't across the border of Shadowfalls yet. They weren't safe.

He stopped within the shadows of a bush, small droplets of water dripping from the leaves around them. Pulling her closer until they were only a hand's width apart, he ducked his head and murmured in her ear.

"Stay here. The path ahead is dangerous."

"I know." She gripped his hand tighter. "Which is why I'm coming with you. You aren't facing them alone."

"I can't bear to see you hurt."

"And I can't just sit here and wait for you to pass by inside a coffin!" With her free hand, she reached for his arm and squeezed the hard muscles of his bicep. "If this is the job I was meant to do, to protect our people at your side, then let me do it."

With a jerky gesture of his arm, he brought her attention to the voices in the distance. "It was my mother's job, too!" he cried, a little too loudly, as he frightened several birds out of the boughs and winced before lowering his voice. "And she died so young that I can barely recall what her face looked like. I would die a hundred deaths before I allowed you to break my heart with one."

He cradled both her hands to his chest, his grip gentle, his expression pleading.

But she wasn't someone who could sit on the side and do nothing. She could feel her raw, magical power rush through her blood. Beneath her skin. It couldn't be contained. "You searched for me so I could aid you with my power. Now you must let me use it."

His voice quavered, once again revealing his fear. "I can't."

She held her head high. "Then you should have left me to the mercy of my flower."

"I couldn't."

"You are impossible," she hissed, her pulse thrumming faster when the goblins started arguing louder.

"And you are rather stubborn."

Yet, the fear never abated in his eyes. Pixies might be in danger, but he was delaying his help because of her. Perhaps *he* was the stubborn one.

"Go." She dropped her hands from his chest. "I'll stay behind." Though, she didn't mention *how* far back she vowed to stay.

He pressed a lingering kiss to her palm, and giving her one last regretful but fearful look, he backed away from her before spinning around and sneaking into the shadowed foliage, disappearing from sight.

She stared at her hand in a daze, the warmth of his kiss still lingering on her skin. What had he meant by it? A goodbye? Or something more?

After a minute, she followed behind. But her heart quickly jumped into her throat when she spotted his cloak on the ground, the fabric pooled on top of a pile of brown pine needles and dead leaves.

She gathered the cloak in her arms and inhaled a deep breath of his earthy scent, hugging it close as if it were him rather than a pile of fabric.

Quinn may have wanted to do this alone… But he had to face the truth.

He wasn't alone anymore. And neither was she.

And perhaps, he was about to learn just how stubborn she could be.

Quinn crept forward, keeping to the shadows of the underbrush in an attempt to avoid notice. Two hares rushed past him. A bird twittered somewhere above his head. But the consistent voices ahead kept his attention fixed on the path in front of him leading closer to the enemy.

He had no weapon except a small knife tucked in his boot and the magic nipping at him from the inside, begging for release. It coursed hot through his blood, ready to obey him should he call on it.

And with his other half nearby… He should be able to call on enough magic for whatever must be done.

Perspiration gathered on his hands as he pushed branches aside and continued to sneak forward. His heart quickened, filled with dread and the terrors of the past. Many of the memories he'd tried to suppress over the years came screaming back at him. Green skin. Viscous teeth. Crude laughter.

His mother's broken body.

The light flickering from her eyes…

He couldn't face these creatures again. But he must.

By the time he reached the edge of the tree line, the voices grew louder, unmistakable with a goblin growl to each of the words spoken. His stomach twisted as he took in the four green-skinned goblins, each half the height of a regular human man. They wore a variety of furs and feathers tucked into their starchy dark green hair. And then he nearly retched when he spotted one of the female goblins with pixie wings as earrings through one of her ears. Judging by the shimmer against the light from above, they were real. Not made from glass. But stolen right off a pixie's back.

"Let me go, you green, rotten mouth-breathers!" Cassie screeched from where she was secured to the trunk of a tree by small ropes. His heart stopped altogether. The front of her was pressed against the bark while her back—and particularly, her wings—were on full display.

A group of sentries, both Shades and Flares, were trapped inside a cage, fighting for a way to escape. And then he spotted the Flare king and queen, Gabriel, and Aunt Tamara within a different cage, each alive but captured all the same.

He found no trace of the Red Cloaks.

"I told you to bring the special knife," one of the goblins growled, smacking another in the shoulder. "Can't be destroying those wings with the one you've got."

"I brought it. I did. See?" He held up a long, jagged knife.

Quinn was going to be sick.

"Not that one, you fool." Another smack. "Good for nothing, you are."

The goblin produced a knife from her belt, and without any further arguing, she stomped toward Cassie.

His sister screeched and struggled against her bindings. No one rushed to her aid, not even the hundreds of soldiers who should have been there, those who had been trained for such a situation. The rain had probably deterred them. And now they would be too late.

One pixie against four goblins. The odds weren't great. But he refused to see his sister meet the same fate their mother had.

Quinn sprinted out of trees, covering far too much distance between himself and the other prisoners. He wouldn't make it to Cassie in time. But his magic could.

A hefty amount of energy left him as a magic burst crashed into the goblin stalking toward Cassie. The creature hardly managed a yelp before the magic smacked her into the trunk of a tree. She slumped to the ground and didn't get back up.

The element of surprise was gone, and quickly, the other goblins searched the ground until their attention fell on him. Two of them started toward him while the third remained behind to guard their prisoners.

"I told you 'e was still alive!" the first goblin cried, pointing toward him.

Green hands tried to snatch him from the ground. Quinn dodged in and out of grasping fingers and quick hands, barely managing to stay on his feet when the movement jarred him, and his previous injuries still pained him.

He called on his magic once again, and the surrounding earth obeyed him.

Vines unfurled from the ground, snapping forward like striking snakes. They curled around the two goblins, the vines tangling around their limbs and horns and pulling them toward a set of trees. The vines wrapped tight around them, holding them fast to the tree trunks and wrapping around their mouths to prevent them from calling out to other goblins for help.

However, he exhausted his magic with the feat, and he wasn't fast enough to dodge the last goblin, who snatched him up in his fingers and squeezed tight enough for agony to surge through his body.

In a blur of movement, the goblin pinned him onto a nearby tree branch, his clawed fingers acting as a cage around his body. Screams permeated the air, coming from Cassie and several other prisoners.

Each breath escaped as a quick rasp when the distance from the branch to the ground disoriented him with dizziness.

With shaking hands, Quinn grappled with the cage of fingers. He gritted his teeth as he shoved the hand as hard as he possibly could. But it wouldn't budge.

The goblin's ear-splitting laughter grated on his brain, and once again, he flashed back to the day his mother had died. He'd only been a boy then. Losing his mother and, soon after, his father? It had destroyed him. Toppled him into nothing. Stole his entire world from beneath his feet and ground him into dust.

And now he would join his parents in the afterlife. Because there was only one way to escape, and jumping from the tree branch would kill him from this height.

"Release me!" he hissed. "Whatever the Red Cloaks are offering you, we can come to an agreement."

"We want all of yer wingsies and yer flowers!" The goblin's shrill laughter echoed in the air, and Quinn cried out when the creature grabbed him, lifted him in the air, and flipped him over. "Yer delicious flowers."

Only for its laughter to cease abruptly.

It scowled as it flipped Quinn back over and brought him closer to its face. "Your wingsies are broken. We don't want this one."

Every attempt to struggle out of the goblin's tight grip proved futile, as he couldn't free himself in any capacity. Wind whipped through his hair as the goblin threw him down again, and he landed with a sickening thud on top of the branch.

Cassie screamed again, but the sound was drowned in the dizziness ringing through his ears.

Pain flared in his back, and suddenly he found himself trapped in the darkness of his memories when he'd been stunned by the shock of the fall years prior, trapped beneath the fountain's water with the faintest seed of hope in his arms.

But he held no such seed now.

The agony crackled down his back and through his right wing. When he used to be able to lift it the slightest bit, it no longer lifted at all. It was far more broken and damaged than before.

Shock and pain stunned him once more, rooting him to the branch, powerless and defeated. He was not the king his people needed. Contending with a species larger than his own was dangerous. Even deadly.

And today, he was no match for the goblins.

Cassie's voice was muffled as she attempted to turn her head to shout, trying to wriggle free from her bindings. Other soldiers tried to escape their cages, but their efforts proved to be in vain.

"Quinn!" Briar screamed somewhere below.

No. No. No!

His head snapped toward the sound of her voice to find her standing with her legs apart, her hands in the fighting stance he'd taught her.

But he found no time to shout at her to run when the goblin lifted its fist high in the air and brought it down with alarming speed.

Everything happened so quickly, his mind could hardly keep up. The fist didn't get a chance to smash him, as a ball of gold crashed into him from the side instead. Quinn cried out as he rolled over the rough surface of the branch, grasping in vain at the bark and leaves to keep himself from falling.

But he ended up tumbling over the side of the branch and plummeting toward the forest floor.

The ground came at him at an alarming rate, far too quickly but not slow enough for his mind to flash back to the day nineteen years ago when the fall had changed his life forever.

He squeezed his eyes shut and braced himself for a painful, and perhaps even deadly, impact. Instinctually, his wings fluttered in an attempt to save himself. But rather than fluttering lopsidedly, they felt strong. Sturdy. Restored.

Quinn flipped over and beat his wings, lifting into the air at the last moment rather than crashing to his death. He didn't skid against the earth like he might have with only half of his wings working but arced into the skies instead.

He glanced over his shoulder, shocked to find his broken purple wing mended with gold. Briar's magic. It threaded through his own, offering him what he originally lacked. It weaved a new half of his missing wing, fixing the holes and the shredded membrane to create something different. Something beautiful. Something uniquely his.

With renewed confidence, he shot upward into the air at a speed even his crow couldn't match. Although he hadn't flown for most of his life, it came naturally, instinctually. He darted around the goblin's head, stabbing and scratching him with his knife. Biting him with his teeth.

The goblin cursed as it swatted at him repeatedly and missed, stumbling backward as it tried to escape the flurry of attacks. Quinn bit him again and then darted out of the way of another swat. After stabbing him in the arm with his knife, the goblin tripped backward over a branch and crashed into the river behind him. The water swiftly dragged him away.

The other two conscious goblins cut away their vine bindings, grabbed their fallen comrade, and ran away, disappearing from sight.

Quinn flitted down from the skies, his feet stumbling across the ground moments before he threw his arms around Briar and spun her in a circle. His beautiful Briar. His incredible wife.

"How did you heal me?" he gasped, spreading his wings out on either side of him to display the gold, shimmering membrane threaded with purple.

Her answering smile filled him with warmth. "I suspected I could when I saw a little bit of gold on your wing after I used my magic for the first time."

"But…but…*how* did you know how to use it?"

She shrugged sheepishly. "Desperation. Nothing more." Her stare turned to the ground, her lips pressed tight together. "I thought the goblin was going to kill you. I don't think I've ever been more terrified in my life."

A shuddering breath escaped him as he lifted her chin and gazed deeply into her eyes, trying to express the gratitude swelling within his soul for what she had done for him. She'd gifted his flight back to him. She'd made him whole again. She'd done something for him that he never thought possible.

She'd given back his freedom.

"Thank you," he rasped.

The words were inadequate. They hardly did his gratitude justice, hardly expressed the deepest emotion burning in his soul.

"Cut me loose already!" Cassie cried out, startling them apart.

Quinn's momentary fluster over having witnesses for a private moment transitioned into worry and then relief. He rushed over to his sister first and cut her bindings while Briar freed her family and his aunt from one of the cages. Tamara looked ruffled, her hair a disorderly mess. But otherwise, she'd survived intact.

Just as they broke the lock on the cage housing the sentries, Matthias flew into the clearing with dozens of winged soldiers at his back. One by one, soldiers landed on the branches or the ground, some of them hovering in the air.

"Where were you?" Quinn accused. His guard should have been by his side the moment he'd dropped off that cliff into the river. "How did you escape while others did not?"

Matthias grimaced. "You were my priority, Your Highness. I went after you, but then I got trapped by the rain."

As did we.

He couldn't fault his second in command for it, no matter how frustrated it left him. Good people had almost died at the hands of goblins.

But if there was anything this terrible situation provided him with, it was peace. The Flare royal family was innocent. Otherwise, the goblins wouldn't have captured them. He could trust them. He knew it now.

"What happened to the Red Cloaks?" he demanded.

The man dipped his head. "Several bodies were left behind, but the others dragged everyone else across the barrier. The goblins were stuffing pixies in cages before anyone could blink in surprise."

"The goblins were already waiting! This plan was deliberate. Thought out."

"No one could see this coming, sire."

Quinn clenched his fists as he realized his people weren't safe. Not until these Red Cloaks were dealt with. "I want guards patrolling Shadowfalls around the clock. Three to each group, that way nothing can slip through the cracks. And I want a thorough investigation. Find out where these enemies are coming from and where they are going. Follow their tracks—"

"The rain washed all tracks away, sire."

His jaw began to ache from clenching so hard. The Red Cloaks had planned this. And they had gotten so very close to winning.

At this point, he trusted very few people. If he must lead the investigation himself, then so be it.

He approached the other royal family, to which King Florian immediately reached for him and shook his hand gratefully. "The Red Cloaks came from each side. We are both infiltrated."

"I was worried about that."

"I'll investigate as well on our end. Our enemies can't run free anymore."

"I'll do it, Father." Gabriel, Briar's brother, stepped forward with a look of determination in his eyes. He swept his damp blond curls out of his face and retrieved his sword, which was sticking out of the dirt next to several others lodged point-first in the ground. "I'll leave no stone unturned."

Florian nodded his head toward Briar. "Your coronation must be soon. We need that extra barrier around our kingdoms."

Briar cast Quinn a confused glance filled with uncertainty. She was still unfamiliar with their customs, but Gabriel was right. They could wait no longer.

"Two weeks," Quinn answered, turning back to the Flares. He would have to teach her more of her magic, but… "She'll be ready."

CHAPTER THIRTEEN

QUINN SLAMMED THE DOOR to the palace closed with frustration in each of his movements. He gritted his teeth, balling his hands into fists as he stalked through the large building. He passed servant after concerned servant curtsying or dipping their heads in acknowledgement, and then he stomped out onto the back patio. Cassie and Aunt Tamara sat beside a billowing fire pit playing a board game with one another.

His sister glanced up from where she was bundled beneath a thick blanket, her face still pale from the ordeal several days ago. Dark circles rested beneath her eyes as if she hadn't slept well, her gaze far away as if she were still bound to the tree with the goblin threat at her back.

It hurt seeing her so…defeated. His spirited, confident sister was reduced to ashes following a terrifying ordeal. She was several years older than him and, therefore, remembered their mother's passing better than he did.

He could guess the ordeal had been more traumatic for her.

"What news do you have?" his aunt asked, concern resting in her eyes.

He glanced from his aunt to Cassie and back to his aunt. Considering the state of his sister, he didn't want to say anything in front of her.

"It's all right," Cassie said with a nod as if guessing his thoughts. "I want to hear what you've turned up."

Slumping onto a cushioned chair, he sighed as he rested his chin against his balled fist. "Nothing. Nothing at all. The best I can do is trace the deceased Red Cloaks back to their families. But their families were shocked when they learned of their involvement." He sighed again. "We've searched these houses from top to bottom, but we can't find anything to further our investigation. They've hidden their tracks. Hidden them well."

Cassie ran her hands up and down her arms, a haunted look in her eyes as she stared into the heated flames. "Then you must capture one of these Red Cloaks alive. To get more information out of them."

Quinn scrubbed his hands through his hair with the vex of frustration. "I can't just wait for them to attack again. Someone might get hurt." He cleared his throat and waited for the thick emotion to unclog before speaking again. "You two almost got killed. My own family. I could not bear the thought…"

Although Aunt Tamara had become more distant in recent years as he'd grown up, she was still family. And although Cassie was older than him, it was his duty to protect her.

"This family has known nothing but loss," Tamara murmured, staring distantly into the flames. "If only my husband were still alive…"

She trailed off, but what he knew about his family's history filled in the gaps. Her husband, who was also his uncle, had been next in line to inherit the magic. But he'd died in battle with the goblins, and his father had inherited the power instead.

The fire crackled and popped in the momentary silence filling the darkness of the back patio. Without a word, Cassie rubbed his back soothingly, and it did wonders to calm the anxiety raging in his soul.

"I'm sure this has been hard on you." His sister gave his arm a pat. "I've never seen you so stressed than in the last several months. You deserve a break."

"You know I can't rest until this is over. It would be a selfish thing to do."

Another pat on his arm. "You are only one person, Quinn." A pause. And then, "Have you been training Briar to use her magic? If she can erect the second barrier, you will be able to breathe easier."

He nodded. "I haven't had as much time to train her as I would like. We're working on familiarizing her with her magic by creating small spheres of protection, by weaving figments of light. She's a natural. But to erect the barrier? She's not yet prepared to exert so much magic. Without control, without practice, doing so could kill her."

"You did it at age eight," Cassie pointed out.

"Yes, but after two years of learning to use it. Briar has had the magic for a week." Warmth clung to the icy frustration in his chest sticking like burrs on his clothing, melting beneath his awe of her. "But she's incredible. I never expected someone who did not grow up in our culture to catch on so quickly. She's dedicated to our people. She wants to succeed."

"Oh!" someone exclaimed.

Quinn spun around to find Briar lurking in the shadows of the doorway, a look of guilt on her face. How much had she overheard? Probably enough for her to have witnessed his devotion to her in his manner of speaking.

His neck heated, but he tried to hide his fluster as he stood. "Briar."

She glanced between the three of them and took a single step backward. "I didn't mean to interrupt. I heard my name and, well…I should go."

But as Briar turned to leave, he caught onto her arm and guided her onto the porch. "Have you met my aunt Tamara?"

Surprisingly, she nodded. "She spoke to me during the proxy ceremony. I apologize…" She dipped into a curtsy. "I can't remember what you said."

"It's all right, goldenbloom," Tamara said with the tip of her head. "It was a rough day for everyone." And then his aunt's attention turned to him. "Be a dear and show her the gardens."

"But—"

"You are insufferable. Leave. A few minutes' break won't hurt anyone."

Quinn grimaced when he realized exactly how insufferable he might have been. He was always talking about heavy topics. Perhaps it had become too much for his family.

He offered Briar his arm. Together, they meandered through a colorful, orb-filled darkness, following a path through the gardens with enormous flowers towering above them, some climbing over metal trellises and others spread numerously over the ground. He tried to ignore the constant presence of guards hidden in the shadows as if trying to remain out of sight, but it was not easy, especially when he wanted some time alone with Briar.

After they passed several stone statues of pixies, Briar reached up to touch one of the orbs, beaming when it bounced off her finger and floated higher in the night to provide a soft light.

"How is this possible?" she asked with wonder in her voice. "What makes these orbs?"

"They have always been here." He touched an orb of his own and sent it floating higher in the sky. Soft like a bubble, but it didn't pop. "They only appear at night. We think it's the natural magic from our grove that creates them. Our land is fertile for our flowers. The skies are filled with magical orbs. It's part of the reason why so many don't want to leave our grove. Including me. This is the best place for our people."

His heart caught when he turned to find an orb casting light on her curious expression. In the dim, pink glow, she was especially beautiful. He admired her beauty. He admired her grace. Her resilience and kindness. She was everything he wanted in a wife, and each day became more difficult to stay on one side of the line of friendship.

The line had to give.

He wanted the line to smudge and disappear entirely so he could hold her in his arms and whisper in her ear how much he—

No, no, no. He couldn't think that word. It was a dangerous word. He was strong enough to endure plenty, but a possible rejection?

His soul couldn't handle it.

To distract his own thoughts, he nudged her side and smirked playfully. "Cassie said she caught you dancing with your parchment pixie."

Her eyes snapped wide open, and her hands flew to her cheeks. "Oh, pixie dust. I didn't realize anyone saw me." She stared at the ground as her face became visibly more flushed. "I feel a lot less lonely when I pretend I'm not alone."

For a moment, his lips pressed together as his gaze swept over himself and then in the direction of Shadowfalls. He was real. Tangible. Decent company, or so he thought. Did he truly not live up to a paper cutout of a pixie that looked very similar to him?

Rather than feeling sorry for himself, he decided to tease her some more. "I didn't realize you preferred your parchment pixie over my company. Shall we invite him on our walk? I could leave the two of you alone together."

Her hands covered her face, muffling her groan and her next words. "My parchment pixie doesn't terrify me like you do."

His brows furrowed as he tried to recall anything he'd done to scare her. Sure, his power could possibly be terrifying if yielded in such a way. He could fight, but he'd never unsheathed his blade in her presence unless on the training field.

Oh...

"Was it the fight with the goblins?" he asked quietly. "Did I frighten you?"

"Frighten me?" Her head shot out of her hands, and she leveled him with her large, green-eyed stare. "You are thinking of the wrong kind of terrifying." She lowered her voice. "We're married, Quinn. I'm scared."

"Of what?"

"I've never been in a relationship before, and suddenly, I find myself married with little to no warning. I don't know…" She bit her lip as she ran a strand of her hair through her fingers. "I'm not sure where I stand with you."

Suddenly, her wariness of him made sense. Normally, a relationship might progress from friendship to courtship to marriage. Not from marriage to friendship to possible courtship. He could imagine she must feel the same apprehension swirling within his own heart.

His nostrils flared as determination stole over him. Cassie said Briar needed a friend. Although that may be true, he wanted to turn that friendship into something more. He wanted to smudge the line. And if he must spell out his intentions clearly, then so be it. The fear of rejection couldn't stop him this time.

So, he braved his own insecurities and took a step onto the fragile bridge stretched between their souls. "I am rather fond of you, Briar. I would like to court you. If you would have me."

He held out his hand, waiting with bated breath for her to either accept him or reject him. In the tree hollow, she had quickly placed distance between them when he'd first attempted to smudge the line. But what about now? What would she choose?

After a long few terrifying moments of silence as she stared at his hand, her lips pulled up in a smile as she placed her hand in his.

"I suppose you are a much better conversationalist than my parchment pixie." Her smile widened when he closed his fingers over hers. "Talking to you is far less lonely than talking to myself."

"I can do better than simply talking." He spun her around several times, delight escaping her gasping lips.

"What are you doing?" She giggled, her hand flying to her headband as if to keep it from falling out of her hair.

"Attempting to dance with you. Is it not obvious?"

She laughed again as he twirled her around with ungainly steps. He'd never taken easily to dancing, much to the frustration of his tutors. He still bumbled about as if he hadn't had a dancing lesson in his entire life.

"It could be a little more obvious," she teased back before she stopped mid-twirl, her skirts momentarily fanning around her legs. She took one of his hands and placed it on her waist, hers on his shoulder. And then their other hands clasped together.

Step by step, she guided him through the movements, how to move fluidly and in step with a partner, how to turn and twirl her and dip her.

Their laughter lifted into the skies through each of his missteps and his small successes. He quickly remembered why he disliked dancing so much when his two left feet refused to give him the upper hand. But he wanted to make her happy. He would practice for hours on end if only to see her beaming smile directed at him.

"How did you learn to dance?" he asked as they ceased the bigger movements and swayed back and forth to an easier rhythm, the chirping crickets and tinkling winds their melody and the glowing orbs creating a romantic atmosphere in the seclusion of the gardens.

"By watching beside the river." She sighed longingly, her gaze far away. "An orc couple came to the river a few times to be with one another when their clans wouldn't allow the match. And one of those times, they danced." Another sigh. "I do hope they got the happy ending they deserved."

"I'm sure they did." His hand gripped tighter around her fingers. "Tell me about your life before we found you. I want to hear more."

"Oh, there is too much to tell!" She laughed, and the simple sound sparked a fire in his heart. He longed to hear it again and again for the rest of his life. But then she sobered, her expression far away. "It wasn't easy, if I'm honest, what with so many predators out there. Snakes. Frogs. Birds. Everything in between. I learned to forage. To cook with whatever I could find. I learned how and when to hide, and my flower helped shelter me from the harsher elements." Her expression lightened, and a smile lifted on her lips. "But I had so many adventures. I can't say my life hasn't been exciting."

"You must have been lonely." His voice escaped as a dry rasp, barely disguising the heartache over her distress. "Did you have any friends beside Priscilla?"

"Plenty." Her eyes sparked with mischief. "But not all of them could talk. I especially liked chasing the dragonflies around the bank. I found many ways to have fun. Surviving became second nature. Though, I can't say I wasn't grateful when Priscilla offered me a dry, safe place to live for a time."

All he wanted was to wrap her up in an embrace and never let go, to never allow her to feel lonely or scared again. "I admire your strength," he murmured, settling for squeezing her hand instead. "I can't imagine living on my own for as long as you did."

"I'm not sure it was strength as much as it was fear of getting hurt."

He shook his head. "It takes strength to learn to survive. It takes strength to stand up to goblins to protect our people, to protect *me*, when you could have run away instead. You are stronger than you realize, Briar."

She ducked her head, but he didn't miss the blush forming in her cheeks, nor the warmth that encompassed his hand where their fingers touched.

"Thank you." She lifted her head to reveal the sparkle of emotion in her eyes, which only reinforced his desire to hold her.

They stopped dancing, and beneath the moonlight glow, Briar looked as radiant as her golden flower, the silver beams catching onto the golden strands of her hair and sparkling in her green eyes. If they had grown up together rather than apart, he realized he would have found himself plenty of competition for her affection. But fate had thrown them together in the most unexpected way, and even though many hardships had separated them, he was grateful to stand by her side.

His hands glided up her arms and around her shoulders before he pulled her into a cradling embrace. One hand snaked around her waist. The other buried in her hair as he held her as close as he dared. He breathed in the magical flowery scent of her. He felt the silky strands of her hair.

She fit perfectly in his embrace, and more so when her arms wrapped around his waist, her head resting against his chest.

His heart beat rapidly in her presence. His eyelids shuttered closed. For years, he hadn't dared to hope he might fall for Briar if they'd found her. But his heart had already slipped over the edge of his careful reserve and was already falling, anyway. Would it fly? Or would it fall?

He supposed only time would tell.

Not wanting to frighten her again with not knowing what to expect from their relationship, he pulled away first and forced himself to drop his hands, even though he still wanted to hold her, to kiss her, to spend every waking moment with her.

But he could move slowly. If that's what she needed.

"I know you are not nocturnal like me," he said as he took a single step away, if only to clear his head of her intoxicating scent. "So, if you are ready, I would like to resume your training in the morning. We only have a week and a half until the ceremony."

"Oh, Quinn. You will be much too tired." When she reached for his hand and squeezed, his heart stuttered, and it was all he could do to refrain from pulling her closer again and holding her until the sun lifted into the sky. "If I am to be queen of the Shades, I must also become nocturnal."

"I don't want you to have to make the sacrifice."

"I *want* to. You would have done it for me."

Sincerity shone in her eyes. His heart warmed at her dedication to the role and to *him*. It meant more to him than she realized.

"Then in that case, I have an hour to spare. If you are ready to learn."

She nodded, and they moved to a grassier spot on the property to keep her away from anyone's flower and endangering their lives.

They practiced for the entire hour, and over the next week, they practiced daily. Sometimes even multiple times a day. She was a natural, yes. But it was as he expected.

She was not ready to erect the barrier around the grove.

Little by little, she was able to create small barriers, and her control over her magic improved by the day. He focused on her successes rather than worrying himself raw over what she *couldn't* do.

Especially because goblin sightings became more frequent.

The creatures now camped near their grove, clearly waiting for something. A part of him suspected they were waiting for the barrier to drop before they swarmed them.

Which meant he kept at least a dozen guards around himself and Briar at all times. Not once did Briar complain about the extra company. Rather, she made friends with the guards, talking and laughing with them and easing Quinn's burdens with joy and kindness.

All he'd wanted was for her to ease the burdens of his weight of magic. He'd never expected her to lift him out of the darkest of shadows with a smile, with a gentle touch. His heart gradually felt lighter, and his soul seemed to shed the layers of darkness accumulated over the years.

Not for the first time, he caught himself staring at her longingly from where she conversed animatedly with his people, telling stories of her time in the wilds to a captive audience. She sat on top of a tree branch jutting out of the ground, her expression beaming with the excitement of her tale.

Quinn's mind drifted away from his conversation with his aunt and several guards about the safety of the Shades as he watched her, listening to her beautiful, tinkling laughter.

But then his heart squeezed when she glanced up and caught him in the act of watching her, and he quickly shifted his attention back to his own conversation.

She was distracting, and he loved it.

And a few times, he realized with a smile... He caught her looking at him, too.

CHAPTER FOURTEEN

"I STILL DON'T KNOW what to do!" Briar lamented to Cassie as they dug through the piles upon piles of dresses lying on top of her bed. None seemed quite right. Or at least Cassie insisted they were all wrong for the occasion despite how beautiful Briar thought they were.

"Throw some magic in the air," Cassie mumbled with a pin in her mouth as she forced Briar into a chair facing a mirror and pulled her hair up. "Dazzle the crowd!" And then she squeezed her shoulders reassuringly. "This is supposed to be fun."

"Fun?" Briar squeaked, shaking her head, which earned her a scowl from the other woman. Cassie forced her head to remain still as she continued pulling a brush through the strands and pinning them up. "My brother acts as if this is serious."

Cassie waved away the notion with her hand. "Flares are always so grave. No offense. The coronation is meant to put the protection barriers in place. Or, at least, make a show of it. There's no sense in not having fun, however."

Nervousness climbed up her arms in the form of an itch, but no matter how hard she scratched, it refused to abate. "In front of everyone? I can't do this. I've hardly had much practice with my magic."

"Quinn will help you. Our warlock, too. Unless…"

Briar turned in her chair to give her sister-in-law a sharp stare. "Unless?"

The other woman conveniently finished her hair and turned around, facing her back to her as she dug through the pile of clothing for the fourth time. "In our culture, this is the one and only time you or Quinn can reject each other as mates and choose another."

All the blood drained from Briar's face, and her stomach twisted until she felt nauseous at the thought. "I was told the bond is permanent." Well, *nearly* permanent. This ceremony was likely the reason why.

"It is. But our warlock can break it under the right circumstances. Tonight is one such circumstance."

Briar massaged her temples as Quinn's words finally sank into her understanding. The coronation was to secure her position as queen. Which meant the title could still be stripped from her.

However, she didn't care for the title as much as she cared for the man she was bonded to.

"Don't fret," Cassie reassured, prying her hands away from her face to adorn her hair in strands of glassy, glowing orbs. "Quinn is just as terrified you will reject him."

"How could he be? After everything we've been through, he thinks I will reject him?"

With a sigh, Cassie pulled up a chair and straddled it, resting her chin on her arms on top. "Our parents didn't face the ceremony until three years into their marriage. I had already been born. Our parents didn't…get along. They kept trying for an heir, and my mother lost many pregnancies. Convinced her womb was cursed, my father rejected my mother in front of everyone in both kingdoms. Only to find out weeks later that she was with child. A healthy child. Quinn. An heir to the magic. Therefore, they remarried and made it work for a time." She sighed. "*Of course*, Quinn is terrified. He wants what our parents never had."

"Which is what?"

Cassie smiled. "Love."

Briar bit her lip. Love was all she had ever wanted as well. Love for a family. Love for friends. Love for someone special. And besides, did Quinn want love in general or love for *her*?

A knock at the door startled her upright. Her nerves were frayed beyond belief. She could hardly take much more of this fretting.

She rushed toward the door and pulled it open.

And her heart skipped when she found herself staring back at a pair of violet eyes.

"Quinn," she breathed.

He spoke quickly, almost as if flustered and he didn't want to give her the chance to speak. "This has been eating me alive all day, and I can hardly stand it anymore. I can't hold onto that hope. To not know. To be blindsided like my mother was. I don't want to be broken-hearted and humiliated." He held out a bundle of white in his arms, and she took it from him, realizing it must be clothing hidden beneath a white protective cloth. "If you will choose me, wear this. If not, wear something else. That way I can know. That way I can prepare myself. Please."

And without another word, he spun on his heel and disappeared down the hallway.

Confusion clouded her mind as she slowly closed the door and laid out the white bundle on top of the messy pile on the bed. She untied the knot at the bottom and lifted the cloth.

She gasped, and her heart caught as her gaze flitted across the beautiful gown with a heart-shaped bodice, dripping sleeves, and a skirt a deep purple in color that melted into a violet that matched the color of Quinn's eyes.

The gown was beautiful. It was perfect. And she planned to wear it tonight, not a single doubt in her mind.

Again, she rushed across the room and dug into several drawers until she found a green sash, a similar shade to her own eyes. She thrust it into Cassie's hands, almost as if life or death depended on it.

But it wasn't that.

It was love.

"Give this to Quinn. I suspect he'll know what I want with it."

Cassie's lips twitched as if she struggled to hold back her laughter. "You were made for each other." And then she paused at the door. "I hope you two will be able to see that."

And then she disappeared from the room, leaving Briar with the beautiful gown that was clearly Shade-made rather than Flare-made because of the bold, dark colors.

For once, Briar could make her own choice and pave her own path forward. She wanted to accept this relationship, this responsibility, this burden.

So, she took a deep breath.

And made her choice.

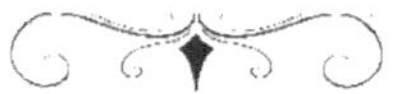

All her life, Briar had owned next to nothing. Surviving and taking care of her flower had been her top priority.

But now she had family. Friends. And Quinn. She had more than she ever dared to dream of. And she never planned to let them go.

Especially tonight.

Tonight, she was going to show just how much Quinn meant to her. How much she appreciated him. How much…

…she loved him.

Yes, she did. She loved him. Perhaps from the very first moment she'd set eyes on her pixie drawing. Or maybe even from the first time she'd heard Quinn's voice and learned what he had done for her. It was even possible she'd loved him as a seed when he'd risked his life to save her own, giving up the one thing most precious to him in the world to keep her safe.

Was she brave enough to tell him her feelings tonight? She didn't know. But she thought her choice of dress would speak for itself.

Briar picked up the hem of her gown, watching as the violet fabric shimmered with each step she took down the staircase of her new home. Combined with the elegant styling of her long hair pinned up, she felt like a princess. Perhaps even a queen. And it was time to prove to her people that she could protect them and lead them at Quinn's side.

If he chose her as well.

The floor creaked behind her. She spun around, heart in her throat as she searched the shadows for any sign of the source. But there was nothing except a wall sconce burning a purple orb and window curtains fluttering in a light breeze.

The breeze sent a chill racing up her arms. Although she knew no one was there, she felt as if she were being watched.

For a moment longer, she stared at the shadows. She swore they moved slowly like a feline stalking its prey. And when she heard the singing of metal like a sword being pulled from its sheath, she gasped and sprinted across the room. She threw open the door to escape, only to stifle a scream when her brother stood directly in front of her, blocking her path.

The shadows behind her ceased moving. Nothing jumped out at her. Surely, it had only been her imagination.

Gabriel chuckled sheepishly, running a hand over his jaw. "Sorry for startling you. I came to escort you to the event." And then he lowered his hand to reveal the uncertainty resting over his brow. "I know we hardly know each other. But I hoped we could change that."

"I thought you disliked me when we met. What changed?"

Another nervous chuckle. "King Thistlethorn, ahhhh Quinn, has been trying to convince the Flares to stay here where it was not safe. I thought you were an imposter at first. Until I saw you use your magic to heal Quinn's wings. He's been lame for most of his life. I know it was no trick."

When Gabriel offered his arm, she hesitated for only a moment before linking her arm through his. She knew hardly a thing about her brother, only that he was heir to the Flare throne.

But now that she was with them, she wanted to get to know all her family members.

"I'm surprised you're here," she said as he led her down the wooden path with more guards than she could count lining each side. The moon shone silver overhead, revealing a beautiful, peaceful night filled with chirping crickets, lapping water, and excited voices by the pond.

"Why? This is a long-held tradition."

She shook her head. "I'm surprised Quinn allowed you over the border. The lot of you are shockingly strict about territories."

Gabriel laughed and gave her arm a small squeeze. "A few events exist where there are no borders at all between our people. Tonight is one such event. It's written in the treaty. Quinn has no say in who comes and goes." Another chuckle, this one darker. "I bet he's writhing in fury by now. A dangerous thing. For a Shade to explode."

"What do you mean?"

He tipped his head to give her a pointed look. "You haven't figured it out by now? Those Red Cloaks attacked nineteen years ago because of what Quinn's father did. His name was Citron."

"Quinn said his father's magic lost control and exploded when his mother died."

Her brother nodded. "He was a bit of a volatile man, or so I've heard. When his wife's half of the magic returned to him upon her death, he was unable to balance himself when he was so angry, and his magic just...*exploded*. It killed a hundred pixies, both Shades and Flares, and started a war between our people. Hence the treaties and the borders. You, Briar, were supposed to end the conflict by being bonded to Quinn. Perhaps it would have, but the Red Cloaks didn't like that. So they attacked."

"But why? To keep the war from ending?"

He shook his head. "The line ends with Quinn. My guess is that they wanted to kill the magic entirely. No more magic. No more explosive power. No more deaths. But then the assassination went sideways when Quinn inherited the power, and you were lost. Half the magic was gone. It wasn't as much of a threat when it takes that much magic just to keep the barrier around our kingdoms erect. There wasn't enough excess magic for him to explode, anyway."

Briar's head swam with dizziness as she tried to grasp onto her brother's words. If she had grown up with the Flares, perhaps she would have known all of this already. The information was new. And it was terrifying. Was it possible for Quinn to explode, too?

But no... From what she'd deduced, from a young age, Quinn had learned careful control over his magic. He was not volatile or wrathful. He was careful and considerate. She didn't think it was possible for him to lose control like his father had.

"And the Red Cloaks attacked again after you came back," he continued.

"I don't understand."

He pointed to her and lowered his voice. "The *threat* returned. You're not safe here, Briar. No matter how much your little Shade makes you think otherwise."

The dizziness returned with a vengeance, and her grip tightened on her brother as she tried to keep her head upright and her feet on the ground.

"Why hasn't Quinn told me most of this?"

"My guess? He thinks you'll leave him. I can see that he likes you. Probably too much."

"Why too much?"

"Because you will die here, Briar." His promise chilled her blood, stole the breath right from her lungs. "And I'm afraid he'll explode like his father did when you do."

When not *if*.

Breathing became difficult, and as if sensing her struggle, Gabriel stopped to allow her to catch her breath. "What should I do?"

He seemed to know a lot more than anyone else did. Surely, he didn't tell her simply to scare her. He was looking out for her well-being.

"Reject him tonight. Divorce him. Give up your power. Otherwise, you *will* be killed. I don't know by whom."

"There has to be another way." Because she didn't want to give Quinn up. She loved him.

Gabriel pulled her into the shadows of a moon blossom flower and lowered his voice even further. "Whatever path you take will lead you to losing Quinn. So give up any notion that the two of you can be together. Either you stay with him, and you and many others will die, you keep the power and live far away from Eliandor, or you give up the power *and* Quinn and come home to live with us in Mapleborough."

"Why can't I give up the power and stay with him?"

He chuckled and released her arm, leveling her with a cold stare. "The power is linked through marriage. If you give up the power, Quinn must marry another. It's how it always has been. It's how it always has to be."

"Then Quinn can give up his power. We will both be magicless."

"That's what the Red Cloaks want. It's the only thing that could protect you both, though a more selfish approach. But he won't do it. Not even for you, the noble prick. Those goblins are out there, and they *will* find us. He will choose thousands of lives over your own." He scowled, kicking a rock near his feet and watching as it skittered into the pond to his left. "No one likes feeling this helpless, not even me. We can either move everyone out of the grove and hide somewhere the goblins can't find us or we can wait until the ugly creatures descend and kill every last one of us." And then he took her shoulder and squeezed it. "This is not a fairy tale fantasy,

Briar. You are a queen. Now act like it. The fate of everyone in this grove depends on your decision tonight."

Briar's eyes smarted as she gazed down at the lovely gown Quinn had gifted her. No matter what she chose to do, it would end in disaster in some way or another. But what was the least disastrous outcome?

And must she truly pay the price for love? Must she give him up to save herself? Or keep him and risk the lives of their people?

With tears in her eyes, she spun around to hide her wavering emotions from her brother. "If you are to be my escort, then wait here."

"Why?" But the lingering smirk in his eyes gave away that he already knew the answer to his question.

She sniffed and wiped her eyes. "I need to change."

CHAPTER FIFTEEN

SHE WORE YELLOW.

Quinn's chest tightened until no room remained for a single breath as he watched Briar round the corner on Gabriel's arm. The audience shouted and whistled excitedly at her approach. Perhaps on another occasion, he might have beamed and clapped along with them.

But she wore yellow.

His traitorous heart dropped to his toes, beating slow and languid as it cracked into two pieces. Then three. And then so many cracks ran through it until it threatened to fall apart entirely.

If only he'd had more time to romance her. If only their people weren't in immediate danger, they could push off the ceremony to a later date. But his haste had led to his downfall. Briar would not be his. She would never be his.

His throat swelled with devastation, making swallowing difficult. He averted his gaze from her to hide the glossiness of his eyes. The green sash tied around his wrist blurred with each passing moment. He pushed the offending fabric farther up his arm and pulled down his sleeve to hide it from view. There was no point in wearing it now.

Cassie stood off to the side, and she met his gaze with a sorrowful look of her own. *She was going to wear it*, she mouthed. *I promise.*

Well, then, why hadn't she? What had changed her mind?

When his broken heart threatened to make him break down in front of hundreds of pixies in the audience, he forced a blank mask to his face and pushed away every bit of emotion until his eyes cleared and his body became numb.

At least now he knew. He didn't have to hold onto hope anymore.

Because it was gone.

When his body was too numb to move, he remained still where he stood on a lily pad floating on top of the water of the pond. The warlock was the one who stepped forward and held out a hand for Briar as she walked across the dock leading toward them. The man helped her onto the lily pad with them, the weight of her added presence momentarily jostling it up and down.

And Quinn still remained frozen.

He was supposed to move the lily pad with either his magic or propel them forward with an oar. He could do neither. His body wouldn't obey him.

Therefore, the lily pad began its journey to the middle of the lake with the warlock's own magic. The only three with power in both kingdoms. If the Red Cloaks wanted to do away with magic, it was dangerous for all three of them to be together in the same place.

But when his cracked heart was numb, he couldn't find the room to care.

"Q-Q-Quinn." Briar's voice trembled as she reached for him. But when her fingers brushed against his sleeve, he jerked his arm out of reach. It was too painful. To be near her. To touch her in any capacity.

"Are you being coerced?" he asked quietly.

Her voice shook when she answered. "N-n-no. But you must understand—"

"I understand well enough."

The warlock cleared his throat, glancing between the two of them with dark blue eyes aged with life and wisdom. The man was born a Flare, but to keep the peace, he lived in Shadowfalls. Quinn didn't see him often except during special rituals and ceremonies, as he otherwise kept to himself in his little temple. But only he could bind and unbind using the ancient magic flowing through his veins.

And tonight...

He would be unbinding.

"Speak your peace now, because in a minute, I will cast my magic over the audience so they may hear what is said."

Quinn remained silent. He had nothing more to say. And his silence caused a wavering sob to escape Briar's lips.

More than anything, he wanted to pull her into his arms. To comfort her. To tell her everything was going to be all right.

But it wasn't. Because after everything, his people would still be without the protection they needed from her magic.

A discomforting pit formed a tight ball in his stomach. He would have to choose another bride without delay. It would have to be one of the Shades, as he would not be able to create a strategic alliance quick enough with a Flare.

And without Briar…it would be a hollow marriage.

"Quinn," Briar tried again, but he held up a hand to stop her.

"We're ready," he told the warlock.

Again, the man glanced uneasily between the two of them before he clapped his hands once, and white magic burst forth and spread over the skies. Now everyone could hear their every word. He didn't dare speak. Not even in a whisper.

He fixed his gaze on the man's green and white robes, and particularly, on the large tome he held in his arms as he began to speak. "For centuries, the Thistlethorn lineage has been charged with the responsibility and power to keep our people safe from harm from outside threats. Tonight, we renew the power handed down from grandfather to father to son and revisit the match that was made nineteen years ago."

The warlock turned to him first, but Quinn spoke before the man had a chance to open his mouth. "If it's all the same," he said in a quiet voice, betraying nothing of his wavering emotions inside him. "I would like Briar to answer first."

It would save him at least some of his pride. Because he could not be the first one to answer. He wouldn't be able to reject her. Not even to save face.

So therefore, he stood with his hands clasped in front of him, head bowed, waiting for the woman he loved to shatter what was left of his heart.

The warlock opened the book he held and instructed them to place one hand on either page. And then he spoke.

"Briar Firewillow, will you accept the charge of power, to protect with your life and your magic, to spend your days as a Thistlethorn bride? Or will you reject Quinn Thistlethorn and the magic that comes with your union?"

Another quiet sob. Her fingers trembled over the book's page. And in the end, he couldn't remain quiet.

Not even to save his pride. Because if he said nothing, he would not get another chance to save their marriage.

"I love you, Briar."

There. He said it. Declared his love in front of the entirety of Shadowfalls and Mapleborough. The audience gasped and cheered. Some whistled. But even the excitement wasn't enough to cut through the thick tension standing between Briar and himself.

She clamped a hand over her mouth to stifle more sobs escaping from her lips. Tears ran unceasingly down her cheeks. Her shoulders shook along with her fingers.

Still, she didn't turn her head to look at him as she spoke in a wavering rasp. "I want what is best for all of us." Another sob. "I reject you, Quinn Thistlethorn, and the magic that comes with our union. A-a-and I hope you f-f-find"—the weeping came relentlessly now—"someone who w-w-will make you h-h-happy."

A small portion of the audience cheered. Most of them "booed."

And Quinn's heart broke into pieces and shattered into dust at his feet.

He bowed his head, feeling the energy of her magic rush back into him and hide away dormant, deep in his soul. His hand slowly slipped off the page of the book, and unable to hold himself together any longer, he spread his wings and leaped into the air, allowing the instinct of flight to take him far away from the pond and closer to the freedom of the moon hanging in the skies overhead.

He had not yet been born the night his father had rejected his mother. But now he knew how much the humiliation and heartache hurt.

And he feared he would never recover from such a devastating blow.

Quinn only got as far as the border around the kingdom when his right wing began flying lopsidedly rather than straight. Alarm shot through him when he glanced over his shoulder to find the gold at the bottom of his purple wing slowly disappearing, starting from the edges and creeping toward the middle.

A startled cry escaped his mouth when the gold disappeared entirely. His right wing fluttered uselessly, and his left wing couldn't keep him in the air when flight required balance. His body tipped precariously in the air, and without his wing to keep him upright...

He fell.

The wind lashing out at him stifled his scream, and he plunged quickly toward the ground with nothing to catch his fall but the forest far below. He willed his wings to work. To lift him into the air and save him from crashing to his death. But they refused to obey him, no matter how much he fluttered and flapped.

He braced himself for the impact of the fall, but moments before he crashed to the forest floor, an eagle swooped down and scooped him into its claws. The impact on the bird's talons alone caused his vision to grow fuzzy.

Moments later, his world faded to black.

CHAPTER SIXTEEN

CRACKLING FLAMES CLIMBED up the logs within the hearth in what wouldn't be Briar's room for much longer now that she wasn't married or bonded to Quinn anymore. The power had fled from her being, and without it, without the bond, she felt as if she'd severed a limb. No longer did she feel whole. No longer did she feel like she could take on the large, terrifying world and win.

The violet brand on her forearm had disappeared along with her magic. It wasn't temporarily gone. It was permanent.

Tears trailed ceaselessly down her face as she tore her gaze away from the flames and to the sickening yellow dress she held in her arms. She hated it with her entire being. She hated the Red Cloaks, too. Even since she was just a seed, they had taken so much from her.

First her home.

Then her parents and brother.

And now they had taken Quinn from her.

How much more were they going to squeeze out of her?

Anger pulsed through every heartbeat, and without further pause, she tossed the dress into the hearth and watched as the flames hungrily consumed the yellow threads. Yellow transitioned into black. Acrid smoke lifted into the air. But soon, the gown turned to ash, leaving nothing behind but a trail of dirty, black soot.

Briar had nothing. No Quinn. No magic. No weapons. But she vowed to hunt down the Red Cloaks and have them answer for their actions.

I love you, Briar.

Quinn's beautiful confession repeated over and over in her mind, which only encouraged the gaping hole in her heart to stretch wider as she recalled the hurt in his eyes after her rejection. She'd betrayed him. She'd betrayed herself. She needed to speak to him, to make him understand why she'd rejected him. But he'd flown away. And she hadn't the slightest idea where to look for him first.

The door on the opposite end of the room burst open and smashed against the wall. Cassie's hurt and anger blazed in her eyes, her wings fluttering with agitation.

"What have you done?" she growled, stalking forward. "I thought you were going to wear his dress. I thought you loved him."

Briar swiped her cheeks for the hundredth time that night, straightened her midnight blue skirts, and fixed her white blouse. "I love him with my entire heart and soul, and I longed to tell him at the ceremony, but not like this. Until the Red Cloaks are no longer a threat…we cannot be together."

The other woman's expression softened as she pulled her into an embrace and held on tight. "You are still family. We will fix this. I promise."

"I need to speak with him. Where can I find him?"

Cassie shook her head sadly. "Perhaps he needs a little space. You hurt him."

Briar sniffed and swiped at her cheeks. "I know. But I had no choice."

"There is always a choice."

She shook her head. "Not this time."

With a long sigh, Cassie pointed in the direction behind her. "He likes to train on the field when he's upset. Perhaps you might find him there."

Wasting no time, Briar lifted her skirts and hurried from the room.

Some servants stared as she passed. Others blatantly whispered to one another behind her back. And when she burst outside into the midnight air, she nearly ran smack into one of the dozens of soldiers guarding the palace.

But they were not Shades this time. They were Flares. Guarding their princess rather than the winged pixies guarding their queen. Her family was nowhere to be seen. Even Matthias no longer guarded her.

The ache in her soul festered as she started toward the darkened training fields, drawing the attention of her guards who followed eerily in her wake. She wasn't used to being trailed by Flares. It was a shock more than she wanted to admit.

She tried to ignore the marching footsteps behind her, following at a distance as she rushed forward. And when she pushed through the winding path and found herself at the edge of the field, her breath caught in her lungs to find Shade soldiers huddled in a circle around someone who lay on the ground.

Quinn? No, no, no! It can't be Quinn.

"What's happened to him?" Briar demanded as she shoved her way through numerous soldiers until she spotted Matthias. But as she broke through the ring of soldiers, the person lying on the ground wasn't who she'd thought. "Where's Quinn?"

Her gaze darted from Matthias's grave expression to the man he trapped beneath his boot, his spear pointed at the man's neck. The Flare swallowed, his throat bobbing up and down, nearly causing the end of the weapon to pierce him with the action.

"This is no longer your concern." Matthias grinded his boot into the man's chest and caused him to wince. "You are not our queen anymore."

"But I am your princess."

The man paused, his lips pressed tightly together before he relented with a sigh. Gesturing with his spear, he said, "He's an assassin. We caught him with his arrow trained on you during the ceremony." This time, the tip of the spear cut into the man's neck just enough to draw blood. "Go on. Tell her what you told us."

All the self-preservation within her warned her to step away from the assassin, but she needed answers.

When he replied, his hard stare turned on her. Not with hatred. But something akin to glee. "I was in the tree. Waiting with a crossbow. If you had accepted the Shade King, you would not be alive right now."

Briar reeled back in shock, her mind immediately jumping to her conversation with her brother. Somehow, Gabriel had known. By convincing her to reject Quinn, he had saved her life.

But what about Quinn?

"Why didn't you kill my husband?" She grimaced when she realized their marriage was over. Because of her. It burned another hole of heartache through her soul.

"We don't want to kill if we can avoid it."

"We?"

Another soldier threw a crimson cloak to the ground, and Briar's stomach twisted at the sight of the red fabric that had haunted her dreams over the last several days. He was a Red Cloak.

"We've never managed to capture one alive until now." Matthias nodded his head toward the man. "He won't tell us anything more."

On the ground, the assassin laughed, but the sound cut off abruptly when the tip of the spear pricked him once more. "I will tell the princess one thing if she can guarantee my release."

"I give you my word," she said abruptly before anyone could deny her. Although she wasn't a Shade Queen any longer, she still outranked everyone on this field.

The others surrounding them glanced back and forth amongst themselves, likely wondering if she was serious or only planned to bait the prisoner with a false sense of safety.

The man beckoned her closer with a crook of his finger, and she leaned as near to him as she dared, still maintaining distance between them when he posed a risk to her safety. But Quinn's safety mattered more.

In a raspy whisper, he said, "I was only allowed to deal with you. My superior wanted the Shade King for themselves."

"Who?"

He cackled, his lips curving into a wicked grin. "The name has slipped my mind." He coughed. "But I can guarantee that if the king isn't dead yet, he's going to be real soon."

As she glanced overhead, she noticed the crackling purple barrier barely visible in the distance. Quinn was still alive.

"Release him," she ordered Matthias.

"But Princess…"

She cut him off with a lift of her hand. Her eyebrows drew together. Her jaw clenched. Never had she wanted to purposely hurt someone before. She wanted someone to pay for what happened. Her entire life had been altered significantly because of these Red Cloaks.

But if she had a chance to fight for Quinn, she would.

Matthias cut the man's bindings, and he scrambled away and sprinted out of the field.

Anger swelled within her as she watched him flee. "Now follow him. I want to know where he goes."

"*You are a queen,*" Gabriel's voice floated through her mind. "*Now act like it.*"

She would. Even if it was no longer her title.

Several soldiers flitted off to do her bidding. Matthias turned to her and said, "Surely, he's not stupid enough to lead us back to his superior."

"Perhaps not. But he's going to lead you back to a place where he feels safe. If you're quick enough to catch him." She knew it because it's what she would have done if the roles were reversed. The assassin would have taken her life and run. As a Flare, he wouldn't be able to get far on foot. He had a hideaway planned out.

"Princess!" a Flare gasped as she stumbled onto the field, struggling for air as if she'd run a long distance. "Princess! I saw it with my own eyes! He fell from the sky. And it took him! He's gone!"

"Who's gone?" The tightening of dread in her stomach told her she already knew the answer to her question.

"Majesty Thistlethorn!"

The world halted. A shuddering breath escaped her lips, and for a moment, she squeezed her eyes shut as she tried to ground herself in calm when panic and rage climbed her like vines strangling the remaining light in a vast pit of darkness.

"Slowly," Matthias said, and she opened her eyes to find the woman gasping for air again.

The woman pointed to the sky toward the pond. "His wing stopped working. He fell from the sky. But an eagle caught him. I saw it. I swear."

"An eagle?" Briar clarified, overly aware of dozens of eyes watching her, waiting for *her* orders. "Where is its nest?" They must move quickly if they were to save him. And a part of her worried over his wing. Why had it stopped working?

Rather than receiving an answer, an eerie silence met with her instead. Some soldiers stared at her with their mouths agape. Others pressed their lips together, shuffling their feet and avoiding eye contact.

"What is it?" she asked, trying to understand their reactions.

Again, Matthias answered. "Only Prince Gabriel rides a golden eagle. He saved it as an eaglet and tamed it as it aged. No one else rides one of the creatures, as they're too dangerous and next to impossible to tame. Either Quinn is safe. Or—"

"Or he's been taken to the den of Red Cloaks," she finished in a breathy whisper. Her head ached as she tried to imagine her brother wearing a cloak, shedding the blood of innocent people. It was impossible. "But he was just a child when the Red Cloaks first attacked. He couldn't be involved."

Yet…

He knew a lot. About their motives. About their history. He'd even saved her life from an assassin. He'd warned her. And he'd been correct about the threat to her life. She couldn't possibly believe her brother was involved. She didn't *want* to believe it.

"Does no one else ride an eagle?" she dared to ask.

More silence. Some of the soldiers shook their heads.

The twisting in her stomach grew more violent as she glanced at the shimmering purple wall. She had to find Quinn. Before the wall flickered out.

No longer would she allow others to make decisions for her. To allow others to decide her fate. It was time to act like a queen. And this time, it was her turn to search for her other half.

She started giving orders to the soldiers. "You two. Follow the soldiers trailing the assassin. The eight of you. I want you to investigate Shadowfalls. You four. Try to find the location of my brother. No one sleeps soundly until we find Quinn. And you." She turned to Matthias. "We search the skies for any sign of the eagle."

The man dipped his head in fealty. "My swallow is an erratic flier, and I'm not sure if she can carry two passengers."

Her gaze darted to the hitching post off to the side of the field, and her pulse spiked as she took in the several birds tied to the post by the reins. Waiting for riders.

Quinn's crow eyed her with beady black eyes, watching her with a quiet intelligence. Slowly, she approached the creature and forced herself to hold her hand steady as she lifted it to touch its beak. It nudged her, almost impatiently, before ruffling its feathers.

For a moment, she felt a shared connection with the bird, and she knew it would carry her like it had carried Quinn. Although she didn't know how to fly it, she'd seen how he'd handled the animal, and she sought to copy his actions. The clock was ticking, and the only time to learn was now.

And she realized... She didn't have to be so afraid anymore. She could do this. She could take charge and be the queen, or princess, that her people needed.

"I will ride on my own."

She watched the bird's beak closely in case it lunged at her as she ran her fingers over the creature's smooth feathers as she'd once seen Quinn do. She continued to move slowly as she untied the reins, placed her foot in the stirrup, and swung her leg over the side of the aviary saddle.

The bird's feathers ruffled again. This time with anticipation.

"Please don't drop me," she whispered, flicking the reins.

Her cry was swallowed by a gust of wind as the bird spread its wings and leaped into the air. She held on for dear life as they ascended higher and higher into the midnight sky, the moon lighting the way ahead.

Soon, the flight smoothed out, and now the bird waited for her to tell it where to go. She hadn't the faintest idea. But if Gabriel had taken Quinn...

Where would he have gone?

"I have an idea!" Matthias shouted over the wind roaring through her ears. He steered his swallow to the left, and she attempted to do the same thing but accidentally tugged too hard. The crow screeched, and she grimaced apologetically, slackening her grip on the reins.

The bird seemed to know what to do, as she gave it full control and allowed it to follow after the swallow. It dipped its wing and trailed the other creature through the skies, climbing higher and higher until the grove below was just a small speck from this distance.

Anxious nerves tumbled through Briar's stomach as she couldn't help but lean over the side of the saddle to look down. One mistake, one moment of losing her balance, could cost Briar her life. And without Shade sentries following them to catch her should she fall, she had no safety net at all.

They circled around the grove and into Mapleborough territory. Briar kept waiting for Shade sentries to join them in the skies or Flare soldiers to keep them from flying through. But no one stopped them. She wasn't even sure anyone saw them, as they were headed toward the palace in a very roundabout way in the darkness of night.

Finally, they descended toward the ground, and the crow landed with a flutter of its wings. Only then did Briar lose her balance, stumbling off the bird and landing on her hands and knees.

But she didn't remain on the ground for long as she pushed herself to her feet and gasped at the sight of what must be the Flare palace and its surrounding dwellings.

The palace was one large tree carved out with twisting stairs and intricate balconies. What seemed like a hundred different floors stood out on the tree, illuminated by silver crystal sconces fitted within staffs of wood.

Mice with saddles scampered across the forest floor ahead of them with sentries on their backs. Several fountains spurted sparkling water within the masses of a garden of flowers.

She would have grown up here. And she wished she'd had the opportunity. With all her heart.

"Why are we here?" she breathed, unable to take her gaze off the palace tree.

"Gabriel might have come here. We need to check." He winced as he dismounted from his swallow. "Discreetly, of course. As Flares, you and I can cross the border without repercussion. But I'd rather not draw attention." He gestured to a darker path with a tilt of his head. "Come. I know of a way inside. We can start our search there."

Eager to see Quinn alive and healthy, she hurried after Matthias, following in his footsteps at a swift pace.

They entered a grove filled with shadows and dark foliage. Matthias glanced around him before he brushed several fallen leaves aside to reveal a trapped door in the ground. With a strong heave, the door groaned open, and he quietly gestured for her to enter the darkness.

Briar clenched her jaw as she reminded herself to find her bravery. So, without too much hesitation, she climbed down the ladder into the darkness until the shadows swallowed her whole.

Stale, metallic air entered her nostrils with every breath. The trapped door groaned shut, and then a torch burst to life behind her to reveal a cavern with patchy walls of dirt, piles of rope and empty torches littering the ground, and a ceiling low enough for her to reach if she were to jump.

The cavern emptied into a longer corridor, flickering shadows coming to life as they traveled down the small enclosure until they reached a fork in the path. She stood silently for a moment, trying to discern any voices or proof of life down either tunnel.

But then the flash of silver in the corner of her eye startled her into spinning around...

To find the tip of a blade poised directly over her heart.

CHAPTER SEVENTEEN

QUINN GROANED AS he came to. Little aches and pains spread across his body as he tried to blink his eyes open. His head pounded. His skull ached. His limbs burned as if he'd struck a hard surface. Had he fallen?

His expression contorted with pain while he struggled to remember what had happened.

But the moment he recalled the events… He wished to succumb to unconsciousness once more. Briar had rejected him. In front of thousands of people. *After* he'd confessed his love for her.

His face burned. His chest ached. He hadn't known such heartache could exist.

And then…

A gasp escaped him as he remembered falling and then getting trapped within the claws of an eagle. Had the bird taken him to its nest?

He squeezed his eyes shut and opened them again, trying to orient himself within his surroundings. He lay on cold, patchy ground covered in dirt. Crates, piles of rope, and *cages* surrounded him, large enough to trap a single pixie. Sconces housing burning white crystals gave away his location.

Mapleborough. He was in Flare territory.

"I'm glad to see you finally awake," a familiar, chilling voice said across the room.

His head darted up, his vision spinning momentarily as his gaze latched onto the red of a cloak, up a slim figure, and then his heart squeezed and dropped to his very toes.

Aunt Tamara stood before him, her black hair pulled into a tight bun and her mouth stretched into a wide, triumphant grin. Her piercing eyes stabbed him directly through the chest with the pain of betrayal.

Despite the weakness of his body, he attempted to reach out to his magic, but a powerful barrier blocked his access. It was as if he stood on thick ice, able to see his magic through the translucent barrier but unable to reach it.

"What have you done to me?" He coughed on a bitter taste on his tongue, trying but failing to push himself upright.

"Don't worry," she replied in a warm tone unbefitting a traitor to the crown, to family. It only made the situation more terrifying. "It's a weak drug and should wear off soon."

Quinn's fists clenched when he spotted a second figure standing a little way behind his aunt. Prince Gabriel leaned casually against the wall with one leg propped up behind him, his arms crossed over his chest. He looked bored, as if he wanted to leave to seek out more interesting entertainment.

He should have known. How had he not seen this coming? How had he not spotted the signs of corruption and betrayal within his own circle?

"What do you want with me?" he asked instead, choking again on the bitter taste in his mouth.

Aunt Tamara took a single step closer, the hem of her red cloak dragging across the floor with her movement. "Your uncle, my husband, was the heir to the magic. But he died." Her gleaming fuchsia eyes pierced him from across the room. "Do you know how he died?"

"In battle," he grunted. "With the goblins."

She nodded and tipped her head to the side. "He died protecting your foolish father. Too young to be on the battlefield. Too scared despite insisting he wanted to fight. If Citron hadn't fought that day, my husband would still be alive. And *I* would have the power. Not you and your empty, useless line."

Quinn's head spun with dizziness, and he fought back the nausea churning through his stomach. "What do you want with me?" he repeated.

The woman inspected her nails and replied nonchalantly, "To kill you and take your power."

A part of him wanted to lie down and give up. To allow his death to transpire. He was tired. So very tired. Tired of fighting tooth and wing to stay afloat above a roaring tempest. Exhausted both emotionally and physically from trying to do what was good and right.

"I thought the Red Cloaks wanted to do away with magic." At least, that was the theory.

She sighed dramatically. "They do. How else was I supposed to get them on my side? To lie to them until I could promise them a better future when I take the Shade throne for myself. I'll just have to convince them that the power can't be eradicated after all."

Wincing when movement pained him, Quinn pushed himself to his knees, but it was all he was capable of without toppling over from dizziness once again. "The magic passes through the male line."

"It does, yes. But I'm confident we can change the rules." With one hand, she gestured to the corner of the room, and he dragged his weary gaze toward the wall where the Flare warlock stood shaking and shivering with his book of magic held in his arms.

"I'm sorry, Your Majesty," the man stuttered. "I'm so sorry."

"Do not call him that!" she thundered. "In a few measly minutes, you will bow to *me*."

Quinn shook his head, fighting through his spinning mind as he tried to make sense of everything that had happened in the past several weeks. "You could have done this anytime in the past nineteen years. Why now?"

His gaze swept the room for anything he could use as a weapon to defend himself. But everything was either too heavy to lift or too awkward to carry. The rope could prove useful, but only if he managed to stand on his feet without toppling over.

She perched on top of a crate and crossed one leg over the other. "After the first attack nineteen years ago, we suffered devastating losses. We needed time to regroup and recruit. Our plan was to assassinate Citron and capture you. Once you inherited the power after his death, you would have been easier to overpower as a child. But Briar's seed went missing, and we couldn't enact our plan without her half of the magic."

"How is that possible?" His fingers continued to search for something to use as a weapon, only to come up short. "One of the Red Cloaks tried to kill me that day."

"He disobeyed orders, which was why Matthias had to dispatch him." The woman huffed in annoyance. "Killing you would have caused the power to disappear, and without Briar, I would only have half the magic. When she returned... Well, it was the right time to strike." She tipped her head to the side and gave him a pitying smile. "I was going to kill her for it, though you made it rather difficult by making sure I could never find myself alone with her. But she conveniently gave it up, passing it back to *you.* Now you have it all. Half of it usable and the other half lying dormant within you."

At the sound of Briar's name, his fists clenched until his knuckles lost much of their color. He hadn't meant for her to become a target in this feud.

"And you?" he asked Gabriel exhaustedly. "What do you have to do with this?"

Gabriel tipped his head to the side, his expression still bored and uncaring. "By allying with us, the goblins have been promised the flowers and wings of those who might defy Tamara's future rule. My people will get the protection of goblin hoards, along with what will soon be Tamara's magic. But many of your people..."

Quinn clenched his fists until his long, black nails cut into his palm. "You are a monster. My sister will be killed. Briar is over there!"

"Briar is a stranger to me. None of my concern."

Next, Tamara gestured to the warlock. The man approached with trembling hands as he opened the book somewhere near the beginning. "T-t-this spell will take away your magic and t-t-transfer it to someone else. T-t-to another bloodline. I don't know if it will w-w-work. The magic has never been transferred to a f-f-female before."

"Stop chattering!" his aunt thundered. "Take it now!"

"He must be willing."

"I will *never* give my power up," Quinn hissed. To do so would get his people killed and put them at the mercy of goblins. "You will have to end me first."

Tamara rolled her eyes. "I should have done this to begin with. Kill him," she ordered Gabriel.

The Flare prince drew his weapon, and his mouth upturned into a wicked smile. "With pleasure."

"Please," Quinn begged, trying in vain to climb to his feet. But all he managed was to scoot backward until his shoulders brushed against one of the cells behind him. "Don't do this."

Killing him would transfer his power to the next person in line. He didn't believe it would transfer to his aunt, as she was a female. But with the help of the warlock... It was likely possible.

He reached for his sword, which always resided in his belt. But it was missing. Gone. Leaving him utterly defenseless against a strong enemy.

Gabriel swung his weapon.

Quinn flinched, squeezing his eyes shut.

But rather than feeling the cold bite of the blade, his aunt grunted, and his eyes snapped open to watch her body slump to the ground unconscious with Gabriel poised behind her, pommel-side of his sword forward.

The warlock collapsed to the ground next when his legs gave out beneath him. Either from relief or fear, he didn't know.

"What…why…?" Quinn asked, trying to speak through his confusion as he watched Gabriel drag Tamara into one of the cells, tie her up with the rope, and lock the door behind him.

"Are you delusional?" Gabriel scoffed with a roll of his eyes. "I've spent years planning this, positioning myself strategically to prevent this from happening. You're not the only one who can protect our people, you know. Besides, I doubt you would have believed me if I had warned you of Tamara's involvement. I needed her to confess to you so you could believe her crimes and bring about justice."

Quinn's shoulders sagged with guilt and relief. Gabriel was right. Quinn might not have believed him until he'd seen it with his own eyes. For so long, he'd felt alone, as if he'd needed to take on the world by himself. Now he realized he'd never been alone. He didn't have to do everything. There were plenty of people he could rely on for help.

"Get up." Gabriel grabbed Quinn by the elbow and hoisted him to his feet. "You still have powerful enemies. Tamara was not your greatest threat."

"Then who is?"

The other man grabbed the warlock next and pushed the groveling man toward the exit. "We have to find Briar."

"Why?" His heartache festered at the sound of her name. "She rejected me."

"Because I told her to."

Rather than drowning in dreary sludge as he stumbled forward on weakened legs, his heart leaped from the dark waters and into his throat. "What?"

The other man shrugged, not bothering to hide the devious smirk flirting at the corners of his mouth. "She was targeted by *several* assassins. I couldn't tell her that, of course, lest I give away my position. So I convinced her to reject you to appease Tamara." He sighed dramatically. "Quite the sob fest as she changed out of some purple dress into that drab yellow gown. It gave her time. But I don't know how much."

"She was going to accept me."

Gabriel rolled his eyes as he located a sword around the corner and handed it to him. "You two are clueless, lovestruck fools. Emphasis on clueless. You left her at the mercy of the man who will kill her."

"Who?" But then the blood drained from his face as he realized the man he'd trusted more than anyone else in his kingdom had lost many family members to his father's magic many years ago. If anyone would have sided with the Red Cloaks, it would have been him.

"Matthias."

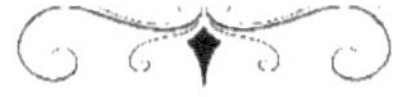

The tip of Matthias's gleaming sword pointed at Briar's heart. So close that if she were to take a deep breath, she might prick herself with the sharp point.

"I'm sorry, Princess." The man's eyes were hard and sharp like his blade, and his grip on his weapon never faltered.

Briar's eyes widened as she glanced from him to the blade and back to him. "But I thought—"

"You thought you were safe with me?" He shifted forward, and the sword touched her blouse. Dangerously close. She stepped backward until her shoulders were trapped against the dirt wall behind her. "I killed King Citron. And I might have killed Quinn, too, that day if not for my orders to keep him alive."

Her fingers brushed against the wall, searching for a weapon but finding none. Not once had she suspected Matthias's involvement with the Red Cloaks. She'd placed her trust in the wrong person.

And perhaps she would die for it.

"Why didn't you?" She edged along the wall, moving slowly, hardly daring to do anything more with the weapon trained over her heart. In battle, Matthias had always been quick. She would prove to be easier to strike down than his foes.

"Despite my orders, I aimed to use him. Get close to him." He shook his head. "Forever put an end to this magic in due time."

"Why..." Her lungs struggled for breath as she tried to take in the betrayal. It was too much. "Why did you wait so long to act?"

He never lowered his weapon, keeping a steady grip and an even steadier stance. "We searched for you for years, and I finally found you several days before Quinn did. Tamara wanted you dead to take both yours and Quinn's power. I wanted you dead to eradicate the power altogether. I tried to kill your flower before he found you. It didn't work. And he made it incredibly difficult for anyone to be alone with either of you to finish the job." And then a wicked grin pulled up on his lips. "Until now when you blindly followed me into the passageway."

She recalled her near-brush with death, and her flower that had almost succumbed to the grave.

"A-a-and you've decided to kill me now instead."

A flash of regret moved through his eyes, the first sign that he owned a conscience. "I do not delight in spilling blood. But I do what must be done."

Suddenly, the marriage by proxy sickened her, and she was glad to have a clean break from her marriage with Quinn if only to rid herself of Matthias's involvement in the act altogether.

"Why are you doing this?"

The man's gaze hardened, his lip curling into a snarl. "Citron's magical explosion killed my wife and two children. I deserved my vengeance. The late king got what he deserved. You and Quinn will be next."

Quinn...

"What have you done with him?"

"I have done nothing. But his aunt on the other hand..." He chuckled and lifted his sword. "I've been deceiving her for nineteen years. She's always wanted the power for herself. I wanted to do away with the magic. The magic ends tonight. And I'll have to be rid of you to make sure it doesn't find a way to crawl back to you."

He swung his blade quicker than Briar could blink. She screamed and lifted her hands to protect herself, knowing they wouldn't do justice against a sharp weapon.

But then a resounding *clang* lifted into the air, deafening her ears. Her eyes burst open to find a pair of purple wings in front of her, the right side ripped and torn, not a single shimmer of gold on them.

Quinn blocked Matthias's sword with his own, his arms trembling as if the feat proved difficult. And then he smashed his boot into the man's stomach, sending him careening backward. Matthias barely caught himself, lifting his weapon again to fight.

"I trusted you!" Quinn snarled. He struck again, and their swords crashed together. "I allowed you to guard her. To be close to her. You betrayed me!" Another attack, this one causing Matthias to stumble.

Briar realized he was placing more distance between her and Matthias by driving the man backward.

"You took what was most precious from me!" Matthias swung his sword this time, and Quinn blocked, the metallic clang reverberating off the low ceilings overhead.

"I did nothing of the sort. My father did. And I am *not* my father." *Clang!*

"Because I have made sure of it by influencing you. By keeping you weak!" *Clang!*

The two fought ferociously within the small space, and she could hardly tear her gaze away when fear of losing Quinn buried her heart in dread. Somehow, she managed to drag her attention away just long enough to glance toward the doorway to find Gabriel holding a dagger in his hand. But his gaze didn't trail Quinn. It followed Matthias.

A sliver of relief took a hammer to her dread, if only to know her brother was on their side.

Briar's gaze darted to the space around them, and she located a pile of metal odds and ends next to a stack of crates. She scooted along the wall and stooped to grab one of the heavy metal objects that looked similar to one of the sconces on the walls.

And then she waited for an opportunity to strike.

The two of them slashed and stabbed, blocked and parried, one gaining the advantage over the other before the tides turned the next moment. Briar held her breath when she noticed Quinn was weak, as his arms trembled and his wings drooped. It seemed as if anger fueled his movements. Otherwise, he might have been unable to stand.

Sweat beaded his brow as he fought with a ferocity she had never seen within him. To protect her. To keep her safe.

And perhaps she should have run for the exit. Perhaps she should have escaped into the night. But she refused to leave Quinn's side when he was in danger of falling. If they fell, they fell together.

Briar stifled a scream as Matthias struck hard enough against Quinn's sword to throw him off balance. He stumbled backward and tripped over a pile of rope on the floor, landing hard on his side.

Matthias lifted his sword to strike.

Quinn struggled to lift his weapon in time to defend himself.

That's when she drew back her arm and threw the metal sconce with all her might. The heavy object struck the man in the shoulder hard enough for him to drop his weapon.

Within the space of a single blink, Quinn launched back to his feet and held his sword against the other man's throat, a menacing snarl on his lips.

"I am not my father," Quinn gasped, breathing heavily. "I will give you a choice, Matthias. Leave Eliandor. And never return. Or face the gallows for murdering the Shade King and other innocents."

Matthias spit at Quinn's feet. "Citron was not innocent. And neither were his subjects for allowing him to remain on the throne. You are naive if you think you can control that power. Someday, it will control you. And innocent people will pay for it."

"I am not my father," Quinn repeated. "I have done nothing but serve and protect. What happened to your family was an awful accident. But it will never happen with me." He nodded toward the door. "Leave. Now. Before I change my mind about your fate."

He picked up Matthias's sword and tossed it to the side, out of reach. But with his shoulder momentarily turned toward the enemy, Matthias struck.

He withdrew a hidden dagger from the folds of his clothing and leaped forward with a war cry. Gabriel darted toward them too slowly. Briar had no weapon left to throw.

Matthias stabbed his weapon toward Quinn. But rather than piercing flesh, Quinn twisted at an angle for the blade to slash through his left wing instead.

Quinn continued through the twist as he shifted enough to stab upward through the man's chest.

A grunt of surprise escaped Matthias's lips moments before his weapon fell from his fingers, and he collapsed to his knees. And then his side. Before the light left his eyes and his empty gaze stared up at the ceiling.

Emotions rolled through Briar's heart. Regret for Matthias and the path he'd chosen. Relief that Quinn had lived through the attack. Gratitude to him for saving her life.

Quinn's weapon clattered to the floor as he breathed heavily with the exertion. His gaze darted frantically about before landing on her. They stepped toward one another at the same time, and Briar threw her arms around his neck.

"I love you, I love you, I love you," she cried into his shoulder, squeezing him tight as if he might disappear at any moment. "Forgive me for rejecting you. I never wanted to. I had no choice."

"Shh, shh," he murmured into her hair as he stroked the long locks tumbling down her back. "Gabriel told me everything. You don't need to apologize."

But the devastation of being parted from him body and soul still struck her straight through the heart. "Marry me again. And we'll do it right this time. Magical bond, ceremony, and all. Give me another chance, I beg you."

His arms tightened around her, and he pulled away just enough to press his warm lips against her forehead in a lingering kiss. "As many chances as it takes, you have them all."

Briar slipped her arms beneath his coat, holding him closer, soaking in his warmth, especially as her body began to tremble from the chill as her shock slowly melted away into safety. Because she was safe with Quinn. She knew it without a doubt. She trusted him with her heart, her soul, her entire being.

"It seems we are no longer even." Her words were muffled in his chest. "Now I owe *you* for my life."

"I'm not keeping score. You owe me nothing."

She never wanted to let him go. She wanted him to stay with her now and for the rest of their days. "I'm so sorry about your wing. I should have acted faster. I should have stopped it."

"It's not your fault, love." He kissed the corner of her eye and then her temple. "It makes no difference because I cannot fly, anyway."

But still, she spotted the devastation in his eyes. Perhaps not just for his second tattered wing but because he had ended the life of someone he had once cared for. She could imagine pain, betrayal, and confusion ate at his soul. If only she could take his heartache away.

"There are still other Red Cloaks," Gabriel said impatiently behind them. "I know all their names and where they are located. But we must hurry."

Don't go, she silently begged Quinn. *I need you to stay.*

Quinn pulled back, his hands trailing up her arms, her neck, and then he tenderly cradled either side of her face. His thumb brushed against her jaw, his long fingernail touching her with a gentle caress.

"You are more to me than life itself," he whispered.

Her heart nearly stopped as he tilted her head up and leaned closer. Near enough to feel his breath on her cheek, to feel the tension crackle between them like embers bursting to life in a blazing fire.

"*Now*," Gabriel emphasized.

He pressed his lips together with obvious disappointment, and she couldn't help but release a shaky breath as she pushed him away with a hand to his chest. This was not the time nor place. But her brother was right. It wasn't over yet.

They followed Gabriel outside to where the birds waited for them. Gabriel mounted his eagle, and Quinn his crow. But then he held out a hand for her. To accompany him. To face this challenge. Side by side. Together.

Briar grabbed his hand and allowed him to swing her onto the bird in front of him. The creature leaped smoothly into the skies on graceful wings. Briar couldn't help but sag exhaustedly against Quinn. So much had happened within the space of hours. It wasn't over yet. But it was going to be.

And that small bit of hope gave her enough drive to see it through.

CHAPTER EIGHTEEN

THEY'D INCARCERATED TWO dozen people directly involved with the Red Cloaks or heavily affiliated with them. Though, Quinn spared the Flare warlock when Tamara had forced his hand. Over the next week, he learned who his enemies had been and who was on his side.

He couldn't help but feel genuine remorse for what the Red Cloaks had undergone in the past at his father's accidental hand. He showed each of them mercy according to their crimes, giving them a similar choice he'd given Matthias—to leave Eliandor and never return or face their punishment befitting their misdeeds. Many left. A few of them stayed, if for family and nothing else.

And without his aunt's direct involvement with the goblins, the creatures had fled beneath the threat of war rather than sticking around for a promise that couldn't be fulfilled now that Tamara was locked in the Mapleborough dungeon.

Quinn had been too close to the situation, considering his family had been involved with the Red Cloaks. Therefore, he'd entrusted her punishment to Gabriel. The man had sentenced her to five years of imprisonment before exile.

Although Gabriel was not sitting on the Flare throne, he would someday take his seat. Quinn wanted the two of them to become friends or, at the very least, amicable rulers. The future took on a brighter note knowing they could work together to achieve similar goals for their people.

And now that peace was on the horizon…

He anxiously rubbed his hands together, warding off the chill of nerves as he waited beneath a crescent moon hanging in the sky like a silver pendant. The light illuminated the glowing orbs of light in a colorful array of blue, green, pink, and purple floating through the air and bouncing off the surface of the pond. One of them neared his face, and he gently guided the orb back into the night sky to continue its exploration across the water.

He shifted his weight from foot to foot, scanning the wooden path stretching from one side of the pond to the other filled to the brim with guests for the event. Both Flares and Shades were in attendance, and having such a massive audience burned a hole of nerves straight through his soul.

Because he feared another rejection.

Quinn adjusted the green sash he wore tied in a knot around his neck like a cravat. The color of Briar's eyes. Burned into his memory from the first moment she'd opened them. It represented a second chance. A new beginning. A clean start. Because the first start had been too rough to endure.

"Oh, stop fidgeting, will you?" Cassie murmured from where she stood beside the wedding arch situated on top of the lily pad waiting at the outer banks of the pond. She adjusted the green sash around his neck and smoothed the wrinkles of his black tunic embroidered with green thread to match the sash. "She will come."

"Yes, but she also came last time and look how that turned out."

"True." She patted his shoulder and smoothed a flyaway hair around his temple. "But this time, this is her choice."

"Perhaps that's what terrifies me the most." What if he wasn't good enough for her? What if he wasn't what she wanted? Especially now with two tattered wings instead of one?

However, he didn't hide them tonight. He was not ashamed of his wings. Each injured wing represented a sacrifice for Briar's life, and he was proud to show them off. Because it also represented just how much he loved that woman.

His breath caught in his lungs. His heart snagged on wavering emotion. First, he caught a glimpse of Briar's golden hair draped beautifully over one shoulder from where she ventured toward him on both her father's and brother's arms.

And then he smiled.

She was wearing his dress.

The sight of Quinn's smile weakened Briar's knees. So much that for a single moment, she found it difficult to hold herself upright and was grateful for the additional support on either side of her. His piercing violet eyes watched her, never breaking contact as he waited for her to approach.

Her betrothed looked magnificent with his long black tunic tucked beneath a gleaming black belt, the fabric embroidered with green, leafy designs along the edges of the neck, sleeves, and bottom hem. He wore half his hair tied back with a woven black crown resting over his brow. A single purple gem lay within the symbol of his status as the Shade King, beautifully complementing the hue of his purple-gray skin.

She wore no such crown herself, but one similar to his sat on a pillow beside the warlock, who also stood on the lily pad beside Quinn.

It was waiting.

For *her*.

For the future Shade Queen.

Releasing a trembling breath, she allowed her father and brother to escort her onto the lily pad with her mother trailing behind as a witness to the nuptials. She lifted her dress just enough to prevent the purple and black hem from getting wet with the single step toward her new future.

And when Quinn held out a hand to her, she placed her fingers in his with an accompanying smile so wide that it rivaled the silver grin hanging above them in the night sky.

"I do!" she blurted, but then she clamped her hand over her mouth when she realized she'd rehearsed her line out loud. A rumble of laughter burst to life around her when she realized the entire audience could hear her, the warlock's power already activated.

Quinn's handsome smirk grew across his face, and her knees weakened once more, especially when his grip tightened on her hand as he pulled her closer. "I suppose that answers my question on what your choice will be tonight."

"And the dress didn't?"

Although he didn't reply to her comment, he took her in with a sweep of his gaze, his eyes sparking with appreciation. Her cheeks heated beneath his scrutiny. Not so much from embarrassment as it was from the fluster of excitement and happiness. In just a few minutes, they would be bonded again. For real this time. Because although it had been real previously, this time it felt more legitimate when she was more than barely conscious for the ceremony.

Her handsome husband-to-be-again flicked his wrist, and his magic propelled the lily pad slowly toward the middle of the pond. Her grip tightened on his hand to keep herself from losing her balance with the movement. When it reached the center of the pond, it slowed to a stop.

The glowing orbs surrounding them stole the breath from her lungs. She reached out to touch a pink orb floating her way, enjoying the bubble-like texture sturdy enough to keep from breaking with the contact.

Beautiful. Everything about Shadowfalls was beautiful. And she knew this was exactly where she belonged.

After the two of them placed a hand on the warlock's open book, the man glanced back and forth between them and cleared his throat. "Briar Firewillow, will you accept the charge of power, to protect with your life and your magic, to spend your days as a Thistlethorn bride? Or will you reject Quinn Thistlethorn and the magic that comes with your union?"

They were the same words that had inspired weeping the last time she'd heard them uttered from the man's mouth. Beside her, Quinn stiffened, waiting for her answer. But she already knew what it was going to be. Instead of grieving sadness, it inspired a billow of happy flames inside her.

"I do. I accept Quinn Thistlethorn as my husband and partner, to share the magic our union brings, to serve and protect our people with our every breath."

The tension melted from Quinn's shoulders, and he lifted her free hand to kiss her fingers and then her palm.

Continuing, the warlock turned to Quinn next and asked, "And do you, Quinn Thistlethorn, take Briar Firewillow as your wife, to offer her half of your power, to serve and protect at your side for the rest of your days?"

"I do," he answered quickly. "I accept Briar Firewillow with every beat of my heart and every yearning of my soul."

The warlock nodded as he reached for the crown resting on the pillow and placed it over her brow. "Then I bind you as one. As spouses. Bondmates. Partners in magic. King and Queen Quinn and Briar Thistlethorn."

A sudden rush of power crashed into her like a gust of wind. Her familiar violet, leafy design re-etched itself across her forearm to match the color of Quinn's eyes. The magic she had only held for a brief time surged back into her, permanent now rather than temporary.

Stronger than ever, she felt her connection to Quinn grow inside her body and soul, unlike what they had shared only a week prior. It was binding. Permanent. And completely and wholly welcome.

"Turn around," she ordered Quinn.

A flash of excitement, of hope, burned in his eyes as he did as she asked. Taking a deep breath, she reached within herself for her vast well of magic. Rather than coming up dry like it would have minutes prior, the magic jumped into her hands with eager anticipation.

Carefully, she dragged her finger along the torn and shredded outline of his wings, and her magic followed as a golden shimmer in its wake. Slowly at first. But then the gold clung onto the edges of his wings and grew steadier by the moment. Her magic threaded his left wing back together and added additional membrane onto the right.

Finally, he lifted his wings, and they fluttered in a stunning collage of violet and gold. Whole and complete. Beautiful. Magical.

With tears of gratitude and happiness streaming down his face, Quinn reached for her hand, and together they shot a stream of purple and gold magic heavenward.

The barriers from their magic settled into place around the grove, stronger than ever and offering sturdy, unyielding protection to their people. Flecks of violet and gold shimmered down from the skies like flakes of snow. The audience gasped and exclaimed with delight, children chasing the flecks and spinning within their glistening light.

"Can you create your own wings?" Quinn glanced at her bare back and then his wings behind him.

But even though she had only had the power for a short time, she knew such a thing was not possible.

She shook her head. But not with regret. Because the skies were not out of reach for her. Not completely.

He moved to stand behind her with her back to his chest, strands of his hair tickling her cheek. Her heart picked up as he lifted her arms beneath his, holding them out on either side of them.

All at once, the roar of the crowd dulled to a quiet murmur in the back of her mind. Her surroundings disappeared until only the glowing orbs and shimmering magic remained, reflecting purple, blue, and gold off the surface of the dark water. For a moment, only she and Quinn existed. The heat emanating from his chest. The gentle touch of his hands beneath hers. His quiet breath teasing her skin.

And the barest brush of his lips against her ear sent a pleasant shiver through her body, awakening her magic, awakening all her senses.

Quinn. It was always meant to be Quinn.

He murmured quietly in her ear, the faintest exhale on his breath carrying his words. "Let me be your wings."

As he placed his foot beneath hers and wrapped an arm around her waist, she knew that she trusted him. With her entire heart and soul. He would not let her fall.

With a flutter of his wings, they darted into the air, smooth and quick and faster than she'd anticipated. She gasped, clinging tightly onto Quinn when the ground disappeared so suddenly beneath her feet.

But after a moment…

Delighted laughter escaped her at the rush of pure exhilaration. Wind whipped through her hair. Trees, flowers, and people passed by in the most incredible dizzying blur. She held her arms out on either side of her, keeping one of her feet steady on top of Quinn's to maintain her balance.

It felt as if she were flying.

"Throw some magic in the air," Cassie had said what felt like a lifetime ago. *"Dazzle the crowd! This is supposed to be fun."*

Her heart climbed to her throat as the energy of excitement coursed through her. She placed her trust more fully in Quinn as she coaxed his arms from her waist, held onto only one of his hands, and leaned forward with her other arm outstretched. He seemed to understand her desire as he flitted closer to the surface of the pond, near enough for her to spot the sparkling shimmer of his wings in the reflection of the water.

She leaned even closer to the surface before reaching for the magic raging within her. Her fingers trailed through the water, and her magic shot upward like geysers exploding from a fountain.

The effect was dazzling when her magic caught onto the silky strands of water. The audience shouted excitedly as the light reflected across the geyser wall, creating a shimmering rainbow over their heads. A symbol of hope for a brighter future between their kingdoms. Hope for safety. Hope for happiness.

Briar giggled as Quinn pulled her closer and used the waterworks as a distraction to flit them away from the crowds unnoticed. They soared through the trees, twisting and turning around obstacles in their path until they reached a quiet stream parting around a single boulder almost as large as her.

Wildflowers climbed across the banks of the stream, secluded and private when surrounded by dozens of towering trees spaced out just enough to let in a sliver of moonlight.

Quinn landed on top of the boulder, and before she managed to gain her balance, he cradled her face in his warm hands and pulled her in for a kiss.

Her eyes flashed open in surprise, but then she quickly melted into him and returned his kiss with equal affection. Her hands braced against his strong, sturdy chest. And slowly, she trailed her fingers over his shoulders and wrapped her arms around his neck, pulling him closer, feeling the warmth of his body seep into her.

She dug her fingers into the strands of his silky black hair, releasing a soft sigh as his hands moved to her waist, his grip tightening on her as if he never wanted to let her go.

In such a short time, she'd met and fallen in love with the soul who was meant to be hers forever. Quinn

Thistlethorn. King of the Shades. The one her heart yearned for, who she never wanted to be parted from again.

"I love you, Quinn," she murmured against his lips between kisses.

A sigh escaped him as his sweet kisses shifted to her jaw, and then he pressed a lingering kiss beneath her ear, whispering, "I love you, Briar. Time nor distance could keep me away from you. And now that you're here in my arms…" He kissed her cheek and then the corner of her mouth. "I'm never letting you go."

"I think that sounds like the perfect plan to me."

And then she kissed him again, reveling in the warmth and safety he offered with his mere presence alone. Within the space of a few weeks, she'd gained family, friends, a home, and someone special to share it all with. She had never felt more blessed, more alive, than she had since Quinn had found her parched and dying while trapped inside that house.

A new beginning was exactly what she'd needed.

And she looked forward to discovering what adventures lie in wait for her with Quinn at her side.

CHAPTER NINETEEN

THE NEXT SPRING, Briar's heart swelled with emotion, unshed tears prickling behind her eyes. Beside hers and Quinn's flowers, a new seedling sprouted from the earth. Green leaves unfurled from gentle stems. And sitting at the very top was a single bud waiting to unfurl its petals to the waiting sunlight.

An Evening Petal blossom.

For their little boy, Lysander.

Beside her, Quinn reached for her hand and gave it an anxious squeeze. Ever since they'd planted the seed to finish growing within the ground rather than her womb, he'd been a fretful mess trying to make their child's emergence as smooth as possible.

She glanced toward the horizon to find the sky growing lighter with each passing minute. Sunrise was almost upon them. Should Lysander find himself ready to emerge, they would meet him today. Finally.

Gathered around them were her parents and brother, Cassie, and several other friends and distant relatives. Each of them were just as eager to meet the next heir to the Shade throne, the first child to sprout within each family in a couple decades.

The first ray of sunlight broke over the mountains. Briar's heart caught, and she found herself holding tighter than ever to Quinn's hand. The second ray of sunlight stroked the sapling, urging him to emerge.

And then the sun broke free from the confines of the mountaintops, draping its cloak of warmth over their shoulders within the light of early morning.

The sapling shifted with movement, and little by little, dark purple petals stretched upward and unfurled from the green bud.

And then a tiny gurgle escaped from within.

Briar inhaled sharply as she took several cautious steps forward. But then she quickened her pace when she spotted a foot with purple-gray skin kicking happily. When she arrived beside the flower, her heart squeezed with joy. Their son had black hair and pointed ears, and on his back lay two beautiful golden wings.

"Oh, Quinn!" she cried as she picked up their child, wrapped him in a blanket, and cradled him to her chest. "He's beautiful!"

Everyone spoke excitedly as they gathered around to meet Lysander as he gurgled and kicked happily in her arms and, next, Quinn's. He gently cradled the boy in his hands, kissing both plump cheeks and smiling down at the beautiful boy their love had created.

Her heart warmed to witness the pure love shining through Quinn's eyes. She wrapped an arm around his waist, and together, they gazed down at their little boy with their excited and supportive family and friends surrounding them.

Lysander would be the next Shade King. Their line would live on, and so would the magic.

When they handed the child to Cassie next, Quinn spoke quietly to Briar. "I can't believe you were all alone when you sprouted. That you were that small and helpless. My heart aches for you."

She squeezed his hand reassuringly. "I spent many years inside my flower. It took care of me."

"It shouldn't have needed to. You should have been here with us."

And perhaps she might have if Matthias and Tamara hadn't interfered.

"All we can do is make sure Lysander never meets a similar fate."

"Never," he promised.

And then he drew her closer and held her within the safety of his arms as they watched as Lysander gurgled and cooed at Cassie while trying to grab her face. It felt surreal to become a mother, especially after waiting so long for Lysander to first grow in her womb as a seed and then in the ground, waiting to sprout after the frost of winter dissipated.

A pinch of guilt wormed its way into her heart when she realized, now that Lysander had emerged, there was still one more thing she needed to do.

"Are you sure we can trust her?" Quinn asked, flying through the air and fretting for the dozenth time as he held their sleeping son close to his chest, bundled within several blankets to keep him warm against the wind chill of early spring. "Humans are dangerous. We shouldn't take him out of the grove."

"Priscilla is kind," she reassured from where she flew on the crow beside Quinn, a dozen guards trailing farther behind. "She would never do anything to hurt us. I promise."

But her words did nothing to erase the worry growing steadily across his face with each passing moment. Yes, humans were dangerous. But this family was kind to pixies.

As they broke through the trees and into a waiting corn field tilled to the ground, her heart caught with unexpected emotion to visit what she had considered home for most of her life. The river ran steadily down a small slope in the terrain on her left. Fields stretched nearly endlessly to her right. And in front of her lay

Priscilla's cottage, the little girl who had sheltered her for a time, the friend Briar had never known she'd needed.

And as they neared the cottage, she spotted Priscilla sitting in the garden with a sketchbook in her lap while she drew the flowers that had popped out of the ground with the emergence of spring.

Briar instructed the crow to land on top of the fence, and as the bird flapped its wings, the movement drew Priscilla's attention. The little girl leaped to her feet, her eyes wide with excitement the moment she spotted her.

"Briar!" she exclaimed, rushing toward them. The quick movement caused Quinn to flit away nervously, keeping Lysander out of reach. But when she seemed to realize she'd frightened him, she slowed her movements and stopped several paces away from them. "I thought you were dead! I was so worried when I couldn't find you or your flower anywhere. And you've been gone for so long."

"Not quite a year," she replied with a smile. And when Priscilla held out a hand, she clambered on top of her offered palm and allowed the girl to lift her higher until she was level with her face.

"And you brought a friend?"

After a moment's hesitation, Quinn flitted closer and landed on the tip of Priscilla's thumb, still holding Lysander close to his chest.

With a large smile and pride flickering in her heart, she introduced her family. "This is my husband, Quinn, and our son, Lysander."

"A baby pixie!" she exclaimed, and although she seemed eager to jump or twirl like she often had, she remained still as if to not jostle them. "Oh, how sweet." And then she gasped and said to Quinn, "You look just like one of my drawings! You know the one, Briar. You liked him so much that I let you keep him."

Heat burned in Briar's cheeks as she recalled the parchment pixie that had, indeed, looked very similar to Quinn. She didn't dare admit to her that she still had it. Nor that she liked the real one better.

"Priscilla, we will be late if you don't hurry!" Her father's voice echoed around the side of the house.

The little girl frowned, her expression falling. "I can't stay. But I hope you will visit again soon. We will all have a tea party!"

Briar smiled as she allowed Priscilla to set her back onto the edge of the fence. "A tea party sounds wonderful. We will return soon."

With a final wave goodbye, the girl scooped up her sketchbook and sprinted away, her braids flying behind her in her wake.

Beside her, Quinn released a tense breath and loosened his tight grip on sleeping Lysander. "I suppose that wasn't too terrible. You were right. She's different from other humans I've come across."

Her expression softened as she recalled the short amount of time she'd spent with her. "She's a good friend."

And then she approached her little family and wrapped her arms around both Quinn and Lysander, pouring love into her embrace for the two people she loved more than life itself. Quinn's worry lines melted into care and affection as he dipped his head and kissed her on the lips. Joy and happiness sparked through her, and not for the first time, she felt like the most fortunate pixie to ever exist.

Out of the corner of her eye, she thought she spotted the glimpse of a white and pink cat dart around the corner of the house. But it might have been her imagination.

Or, she thought to herself as she recalled Laelynn's part in bringing her and Quinn together. She smiled and kissed Quinn again and then brushed a kiss across their son's forehead. *Perhaps it wasn't my imagination after all.*

Support the O.U.R.

The purpose of the "Hope Ever After" series is to spread hope and be an avenue to support and raise awareness in the fight against human trafficking and slavery. Here are some facts about human trafficking:

Every 30 seconds another person becomes a trafficking victim.

There are 40.3 million modern-day slaves estimated by the International Labour Organization. 1 in 4 slavery victims are children. 71% of slavery victims are women and girls.

Trafficking in persons is now the 2nd largest illicit industry in the U.S., 2nd only to the drug trade. It is also the fastest growing form of international crime. (UNICEF)

It is estimated that the human trafficking enterprise generates roughly $150 billion dollars a year.

The O.U.R. has aided in the arrest of over 4,000 predators, recovered over 6,000 survivors, and supported over 1,000 operations.

How can you help?

- Educate yourself on how to recognize a victim of trafficking.
- Take a stand against pornography, which leads the demand for sex trafficking.
- Pray. Pray for victims and pray for those in the operations who are searching and rescuing victims.
- Buy all the books in the "Hope Ever After" series! All the proceeds from this series go to the O.U.R. to fight and end sex trafficking.

We hope our books inspire you to join the fight against human trafficking because God's children are not for sale. Thank you so much for your support!

"The only thing necessary for the triumph of evil is for good people to do nothing." -Edmund Burke

"Always remember, you have within you the strength, the patience, and the passion to reach for the stars to change the world." -Harriet Tubman

"There are three types of people: those who fight, those who help the fighter, and those who do nothing." -Dennis Prager

Hope Ever After

"Hope Ever After" is a collection of twenty hopeful and uplifting fairy tale retellings. Each book is written by a different author so it can be enjoyed in any order. The proceeds from this series are donated to the O.U.R. (Operation Underground Rescue) to rescue children from sexual exploitation and trafficking. Be sure to collect all twenty, as the entire series, put together, forms a rainbow, a symbol of hope and of God's love!

An Ambitious Hope: A Red Riding Hood Retelling by Lucy Winton

A Gentle Hope: A Beauty and the Beast Retelling by Sarah Carlisle

A Silent Hope: A Wounded Lion Retelling by Madisyn Carlin

A Fairest Hope: A Snow White Retelling by S. Lee Poole

A Crowned Hope: A Prince and the Pauper Retelling by Kayla Eshbaugh

A Golden Hope: A Rumpelstiltskin Retelling by Chelsey Noelle

A Beautiful Hope: An Ugly Duckling Retelling by Leialoha Humpherys

A Hidden Hope: A Princess and the Pea Retelling by Sara Elisabeth

A Charming Hope: A Frog Prince Retelling by Ashley Evercott

An Enduring Hope: A Wild Swans Retelling by Jes Drew

A Cascading Hope: A Little Mermaid Retelling by Yakira Goldsberry

A Midnight Hope: A Cinderella Retelling by Stefanie Lozinski

A Faithful Hope: A Blue Bird Retelling by DaLeena Taylor

A Gracious Hope: A Sleeping Beauty Retelling by Robyn Sarty

A Wishful Hope: An Aladdin Retelling by Sarah Beran

A Healing Hope: A Rapunzel Retelling by Selina De Luca

A Wingless Hope: A Thumbelina Retelling by Sydney Winward

A Secret Hope: A Goose Girl Retelling by Scarlett Luna Strange

A Frigid Hope: A Snow Queen Retelling by Amanda Thompson

A Last Hope: A King Thrushbeard Retelling by Verity Sandahl

ABOUT THE AUTHOR

Sydney Winward is an award-winning fantasy and paranormal romance author who dabbles in the occasional historical fiction. She loves building complex worlds filled with magic, strong characters, and emotional stories.

Sydney is the author of the Sunlight and Shadows Series and the best-selling Bloodborn Series, and when she's not writing, she's reading, thinking about stories, or going on adventures with her children. She lives in Utah with her husband and three amazing kids.

www.sydneywinward.com